Nevermore

NEVERMORE

Marie Redonnet

TRANSLATED BY JORDAN STUMP

University of Nebraska Press

Lincoln & London

Copyright © by P.O.L., 1994 Trans-
lation copyright © 1996
by the University of Nebraska Press
Manufactured in the United States
of America. ♾ The paper in
this book meets the minimum re-
quirements of American
National Standard for Information
Sciences – Permanence
of Paper for Printed Library Mater-
ials, ANSI Z39.48-1984.
Library of Congress Cataloging-in-
Publication Data
Redonnet, Marie. [Nevermore. English]
Nevermore /
Marie Redonnet ; translated by
Jordan Stump.
p. cm. – (European women writers
series)
ISBN 0-8032-3912-2
(alk. paper). – ISBN 0-8032-8959-6
(pbk. : alk. paper)
I. Stump, Jordan, 1959–   . II. Title.
III. Series. PQ2678.E285N48
1996 843'.914–dc20 96-1288 CIP

Translator's Introduction

The world depicted in Marie Redonnet's novels is at once unfailingly strange and strangely familiar: a perfectly plausible world that is haunted by a very everyday sort of entropy, but that never quite conforms to our own. Or perhaps it conforms too closely to our own, magnifying certain details of its makeup – the unlikely coincidence, the unexpected connection, the hidden underside – until they evoke something we have not yet *seen*, but might at some point have *glimpsed.*

Such is the world of *Nevermore*, set in a place that closely resembles (but is not) the West Coast of the United States. This is unmistakably, and quite deliberately, an outsider's construction of the American West: a West where accounts are settled in francs, a West marked by both volcanoes and disused concentration camps, a West in which one finds such quintessentially French conveniences as the *buvette* (a small, modest, but not inelegant sort of café, common at French tourist sites) and the *pissotière* (a rather rudimentary public urinal, now vanished from the streets of Paris). This is not quite the true West, yet the American reader might well be expected to have glimpsed, at one time or another, something like the raw corruption of San Rosa or the bland revisionism of its sister-city, Santa Flor.

Readers familiar with the novels of Marie Redonnet will find in *Nevermore* all the hallmarks of her unique vision: an insistence on repetition, duality, and duplicity, a meditation on the dangers of identification, an examination of the perils and the possibilities of writing, a style of bewildering simplicity, understated power, and offhanded humor, and most important of all, perhaps, a faith in the rare, frail, but incalculably precious ability to transcend the omnipresent darkness and to start anew. *Nevermore* – the novel or the word itself – implies an end, perhaps a death, but also (or therefore) a beginning and a rebirth.

Marie Redonnet was born in 1948. Trained as a teacher, she turned to writing in her late thirties. Her first publication was a cycle of haiku-like poems, *Le Mort et Cie* (1985), soon followed by a collection of interrelated short stories, *Doublures* (1986), but she is best known for her novels and novellas (*Splendid Hôtel, Forever Valley, Rose Mélie Rose, Silsie, Candy Story, Nevermore*) and her plays (*Tir et Lir, Mobie-Diq, Seaside, Le Cirque Pandor, Fort Gambo*). *Nevermore* is the fifth of Redonnet's novels to be published in translation by the University of Nebraska Press.

I would like to thank those whose help and encouragement made this translation possible: Warren Motte, Tom Vosteen, Eleanor Hardin, and Marie Redonnet.

Nevermore

In memory of Danilo Kis

This transfer to San Rosa, on the west coast, just next to the border, was not what Willy Bost had dreamt of. But he wants to forget what he had dreamt of, just as he wants to forget the past. On the first page of the notebook he bought just before he left for San Rosa, he wrote in red ink: *It is forbidden to remember the past. It is forbidden to compare the present with what I had dreamt of.* He chose that particular notebook because it fit into the inside pocket of his jacket, so that it would always be within reach. As if he were going to need an assistant in San Rosa, and had decided that this notebook would be his assistant.

Once famous for its bay and its volcano, San Rosa has become a real boomtown since the reopening of the border. That is what Willy Bost knows of San Rosa, after having read the guidebook. He also knows that no one wants to be appointed to San Rosa. They must have sent him there because they couldn't care less what he wants, and because he is considered undesirable in High Places. They couldn't fire him because he had never done anything to justify such a punishment, so instead they transferred him to San Rosa, without regard for his wishes. His wishes, too, belong to the past, and he will have to forget them. They told him nothing about the position, only that he would act as deputy to Commander Roney Burke.

It took him three days on the highway to get to San Rosa. The Pontiac, which he had bought for next to nothing the day before he left, is not made for such a long trip. Every hour, he has to stop and let the engine cool off. It overheats as soon as he steps on the accelerator. The outside thermometer reads 105 degrees. The air conditioning doesn't work. He is soaking wet and his eyes are burning when he stops at the last service station before San Rosa to let the engine cool off and to go have a drink in the bar.

Coming out of the bar, he feels much better. The Coke has already produced its invigorating effect. But he did not foresee that the Pontiac would decide that the trip was over as far as it was concerned. No matter what he tries, even the crank, there is no way to get it started. The mechanic on duty told him the valves were blown and that he would need a new cylinderhead. That was how he met Cassy Mac Key. She has just parked her coupe next to the Pontiac. The coupe immediately catches his eye. It is an old model, no longer on the market. He would surely compliment her on it if he were not so preoccupied by the Pontiac which absolutely will not start.

Cassy Mac Key is very elegant in her white poplin dress, which looks so immaculate that it might have just come from the cleaner's. She notices that he is having mechanical problems, and very kindly offers to help him. It's a stroke of luck that she's going to San Rosa like he is, and that she happens to have a towrope in her trunk. That way they can attach the Pontiac to the coupe. As long as they drive slowly and put on the brakes going downhill, they will make it to San Rosa. The mechanic on duty assures them of that as he helps them attach the rope. The Pontiac being towed by the coupe makes quite a spectacle on the highway. The coupe, with its brand-new motor, tows the Pontiac with no difficulty.

In front of the office of Commander Roney Burke, Willy Bost unhooks the Pontiac from the coupe. It was very lucky for him that the coupe had given him a tow. As he is about to say goodbye to Cassy Mac Key, he asks her for her address in San Rosa. Once he has settled in, he will invite her out to thank her for the favor. She has no personal address, only the address of the Babylon, where she has just been hired as a singer. Seeing her emerge from her coupe in her white poplin dress, he would never have thought that she was going to San Rosa to sing at the Babylon.

§2

Commander Roney Burke wonders why those in High Places have suddenly become interested enough in San Rosa to send him a deputy. A deputy is just what he has been asking for ever since he got there, in order to deal with the new conditions created by the reopening of the border. But they never answered him. So he became used to being alone, and even came to like it. How could he have imagined when he arrived in San Rosa that he would still be here after all this time, and that his only desire would be to stay here forever? It will be San Rosa right up to the end for him.

He wanted to make his office more presentable for the arrival of his deputy. For the first time, he made up his mind to move the files that were cluttering up the office. He has never looked at them. The files, already yellowing, were put together by his predecessor, who was obsessed with files and wanted to leave some mark of his existence behind him. They are all written in violet ink, in a fine, compact hand, without corrections. They are almost illegible. Why did his predecessor keep all those files? No one has ever read them. Apart from his monthly report to High Places, Commander Roney Burke never writes. What good would it do to write down what goes on in San Rosa, when all that is necessary is to read Dany Sapin's *Gazette*, which tells everything there is to know? If there is one thing Commander Roney Burke has realized since he arrived in San Rosa, it is the uselessness of the files cluttering up his office. The fate of his predecessor proves it. He was not even given a funeral oration when he died. He died while on duty, the year the border was reopened. They found him one morning in the pissotière at the Fuch Circus. When the commander arrived in San Rosa, he was ordered to close the case. The order came from President Hardley. There was no disagreeing with it.

All his predecessor's files have now been taken down to the basement where they keep the archives. So that everything would be in order, he added a card to the card catalog and numbered all the files. But then he notices what a state the office is in. Termites have eaten through the floorboards, and the walls are stained by the mosquitoes his predecessor must have crushed. San Rosa is infested with mosquitoes during the rainy season. It is too late to think of putting everything to rights. The only thing the commander does, after having taken out the files, is to put in a second desk facing his own. He also buys a fax and an answering machine.

In his cupboard he puts his bourbon and his medicine. He replenishes his supply of bourbon every month. As he is rearranging his cupboard so that his deputy can use half of it, he notices his hands are shaking. Is it a new symptom? But what will happen if his hands never stop shaking? Every morning, he goes and practices at the shooting range to prove he is still the best. Until now, he has never feared any rival, not even President Patter, who practices at the same time as he does. Despite his persistence, President Patter always misses the last target, which only Commander Roney Burke manages to hit. No one in San Rosa knows why President Patter spends so much time at the shooting range. He is president of the Council, a shadowy man who lives apart from the rest. Everyone fears him and defers to him. They say he has in his possession all the files on San Rosa, ever since the war. So far, he has never opened one. He seems to have no vices. If he has a passion, it is a secret passion. Commander Roney Burke pays no attention to President Patter. He fears no one in San Rosa.

To tell the truth, the only thing that preoccupies Commander Roney Burke is Rosa Dore. Rosa Dore is the owner of the Eden Palace, which put San Rosa on the map because of the movie which was shot there and which bears its name. Rosa Dore plays the role of a singer who, with just one song, "Eden Palace," makes any man within earshot fall madly in love with her. Commander Roney Burke cannot help thinking that the arrival of his deputy is going to disturb the order of his life, at the center of which is Rosa Dore. That might be why he feels so agitated this morning. The pain from his ulcer will not go away, even though he took twice the usual dose of pills. He is suddenly afraid that the volcano will come back to life. The volcano has been dormant for as long as he has lived in San Rosa. Some people even say that it is dying, like the other volcanoes in the chain. Everyone is taking advantage of the lull, as if it were going to last forever.

§3

Commander Roney Burke does not ask Willy Bost if he had a good trip. He doesn't like small talk or rules of etiquette. His only greeting is a smile, which Willy Bost can interpret as he likes. Willy Bost wants to take care of the practical questions first. What garage can he trust to repair the Pontiac, and where can he stay, in this city in which nothing is familiar to him? The commander quickly answers both questions. He knows Drove Wrangler, the manager of the Grand Garage, very well. Drove Wrangler will be pleased to repair his deputy's Pontiac, and to lend him a car to use in the meantime. The question of lodging is not so easily resolved. The apartment buildings in the city center are unsound and rent in the Bay area is out of sight. The best solution would be the boardinghouse run by Lizzie Malik, who was once the acrobat in the Fuch Circus. She has had her grandmother's house restored, the most beautiful house in the city center, and is looking for lodgers.

Willy Bost accepts this suggestion. Rooming in the home of a former acrobat is not a bad solution for the time being. After all, he once had a passion for the circus! Now he is very curious to know how his work will be organized and what his responsibilities will be. Commander Roney Burke had foreseen that question. His deputy will take care of San Rosa, while he himself will finally be able to explore Santa Flor, on the other side of the border. To him, Santa Flor means the old Camp, with its sinister memories. No one ever talks about the Camp, as if it had never existed. Willy Bost is pleased to learn that San Rosa will be his responsibility. That is an unheard-of responsibility for a deputy.

Now that the practical issues are settled, Commander Roney Burke invites his deputy to the Bay Blue so they can get to know each other better. He is very surprised to discover that Willy Bost is not talkative, and that he gives an evasive answer to any question about his past. That might be a good start. Since he does not want to talk about his past, he will easily understand that Commander Roney Burke does not want to talk about his own. They have discovered three interests in common: the circus, the movies, and the ocean. The circus of San Rosa is the Fuch Circus, which no longer has any connection with what it used to be, except the name. Dora Atter, who had inherited it, sold it for a very high price to Gobbs after he had bought all the land in the Volcano area, which up to then was impossible to build on. That was where he had decided to construct his Amusement Park. All of San Rosa admires Gobbs, the grandson of a fisherman who became, by talent alone, the richest man in San Rosa after President Hardley. Now he owns the entire fishing fleet, and he reigns over the Volcano area thanks to his Amusement Park, whose popularity extends all the way to Santa Flor. As for the movies, which, thanks to *Eden Palace*, had once made San Rosa's reputation, everyone hopes that they are on their way back. The Bay area is springing to life now that the Lossfell Company has decided to build its new studios there. They are awaiting the arrival of Tony Landry, who is coming to San Rosa to film his latest blockbuster.

On the terrace of the Bay Blue, Willy Bost cannot take his eyes off the *Moby Dick*, a magnificent three-master with all its sails unfurled, anchored next to the *Salve Regina*, Dora Atter's new yacht. The *Moby Dick* belongs to Gobbs, who gives parties for his friends there at night. As for Commander Roney Burke, he is the owner of the *Mangor*, a little fishing boat which he has made his home. Every Sunday he sets out in the *Mangor* to see Mattie at Angel Cove, just at the end of the bay. Mattie is the former costume maker of the Fuch Circus, who gave up on the circus the day Dora Atter sold it to Gobbs. She moved to Angel Cove, into her father's bungalow, which she turned into a buvette. Only on Sundays, when he sets out in the *Mangor*, does Commander Roney Burke forget Rosa Dore. He could not prevent himself from telling Willy Bost about her. But Willy Bost, despite his interest in the movies, has never seen *Eden Palace* and has never even heard of Rosa Dore.

Willy Bost's last question concerns the Babylon. The Babylon belongs to Dora Atter. It is a former cruise ship that has been remodeled and can no longer sail. It is to the night what Gobbs's Amusement Park is to the day. Thanks to the money she earns from the Babylon, Dora Atter has become the second largest shareholder of the

Fuller Bank, after President Hardley. They say she is the most ambitious woman in San Rosa. Willy Bost is finally learning something about President Hardley, whose name has come up several times in the conversation. He is the president of the Fuller Bank and the governor of San Rosa. The Fuller Bank controls everything in San Rosa, except for Gobbs, who founded his own bank, GobbsBank.

It is time for Willy Bost to be on his way. Now that he has met Commander Roney Burke and is feeling better about his job, he is in a hurry to introduce himself to his landlady. The commander invites his deputy to join him aboard the *Mangor* for a cruise on the ocean next Sunday. He will take him to Angel Cove and introduce him to Mattie. Willy Bost accepts the invitation with pleasure. He certainly would never be able to buy himself a boat on the money he makes as a deputy, not even an old fishing boat like the *Mangor*.

§4

That day, for the first time in a long time, Lizzie Malik told herself that maybe the wheel had begun to turn again for her. That is how she sees her life up to now, as a larger and larger wheel which, after having turned faster and faster, suddenly stopped. That was the day of her accident at the Fuch Circus. It took her more than a year in San Rosa hospital to learn to walk again. She cannot forget the circus performers whom she thought were her friends, and who all turned away from her as if she no longer existed. But if they rejected her that way, it was because her accident was not an accident like any other. She should never have fallen at that moment. She had never felt so sure of herself. She had the impression that her act was created specially for her and that thanks to it she was going to become a great acrobat. She is certain that she fell because someone at the Fuch Circus wanted her to fall. Even though she spent many long days in a deep coma after her accident, she recalls as if she were there the moment when the rope gave way in her hands because someone had cut through it.

In the hospital, as soon as she came out of her coma, she began to shout that someone had cut her rope and had tried to kill her. The specialist who had operated on her said it was delirium brought on by the shock of the operation. No one at the circus had seen the damaged rope. So someone must have taken advantage of the panic in the ring after the accident to put the rope out of sight. Lizzie made a formal complaint to Commander Roney Burke, asking that an investigation be opened. But her complaint was never acted upon, since it was only the effect of delirium brought on by the shock of the operation. She repeated her story to each of the circus performers who came to see her after the accident, and asked them to help her uncover the truth. They all turned away from her with a sad look, as if they thought she was lost forever in the depths of her delirium, never to return.

No one was waiting for Lizzie when she left the hospital. She had hoped, because he had continued to come and see her every Sunday, that Livio would be there waiting for her. Livio was the magician of the Fuch Circus, and Lizzie was desperately in love with him. She had sworn to get close to him by becoming a great acrobat. But the only thing she got close to was the sand of the ring where she crashed. In the hospital, she wrote him long letters telling of her love and also of her accident, calling it a criminal attack. He never answered her letters. But because he continued to visit her every Sunday with a bouquet of roses, Lizzie wanted to believe that she would finally get close to him. When she was released from the hospital, she learned that he had left the Fuch Circus, and had told no one where he was going.

The only thing that belongs to Lizzie is her grandmother's house in the city center. Her grandmother had never wanted to sell it, even after she had moved out of it. When she left the hospital, Lizzie found the house going to ruin. The wood was beginning to rot and the ceilings were threatening to collapse. It would take a great deal of money to restore it. Lizzie admired the beauty of the house despite its dilapidation. She found a plaque in the attic, engraved with the words *Gold House*. She put it up on the front of the house, as if that were its name. She had only one concern from then on: restoring the Gold House. She looked for a job so that she could pay for the repairs. Her grace and her past as an acrobat charmed Rosa Dore, who hired her as an evening waitress in the bar of the Eden Palace. The tips that she earned in addition to her salary allowed her to restore the Gold House little by little. Now she could rent out its two most beautiful rooms. She had put up a notice in the lobby of the Eden Palace. But for weeks the two rooms remained vacant, with no prospective tenants, because of the bad reputation of the city center. And now in just one day both rooms are rented, one to the deputy of Commander Roney Burke, the other to the new singer at the Babylon!

Cassy Mac Key has just moved in when Willy Bost rings the doorbell of the Gold House.

§5

The sight of Lizzie Malik gives Willy Bost a jolt. His entire body shakes. But he soon gets a grip on himself. He remembers the words written in red ink on the first page of his notebook: *It is forbidden to remember the past. It is forbidden to compare the present with what I had dreamt of.* Lizzie Malik is his landlady, and only his landlady. His eyes lose their gleam, his body stiffens. He introduces himself in an expressionless voice, very formally, as if he were in High Places.

Lizzie Malik has set out flowers to celebrate her lodgers' arrival. There is music playing as well, and a bottle of champagne in the fridge. She does not seem to notice Willy Bost's coolness. She is so happy to have rented her two rooms at last and to have two lodgers to look after in her house. She was hoping to be able to bring them together in a welcome tea, but Cassy Mac Key has already gone off to her room. Willy Bost thinks what a coincidence it is to be living in the same house as Cassy Mac Key, whom he met on the highway this very morning in equally unpredictable circumstances. Lizzie is doing all the work in the conversation. She is wearing a lace body stocking with black leggings and a man's white silk shirt. Seeing her look so graceful, no one would ever guess what she had been through. She asks Willy Bost who he is and where he comes from. But he does not want to talk about himself. The only thing he wants is to move into his room.

Lizzie Malik understands how incongruous it would be to offer Willy Bost a glass of champagne, as she had been thinking of doing. She takes his suitcases and asks him to follow her. He says nothing about the room that she had so carefully decorated, or about the patio, which she maintains herself and onto which the room opens. Her grandmother had given her seeds from all the flowers that Sister Cize grows in the garden of the Holy Savior Rest Home, and the patio is already covered with blooms. Both of the rooms, which are side by side, have an outside entry giving onto the street. Lizzie Malik was very anxious that her lodgers have their independence. She reminds Willy Bost that he can use the kitchen and that the food is included in the price of the room. Lizzie Malik would be so happy if Willy Bost complimented her on her house. But he remains stony.

After setting down the suitcases in the room, throwing open the shutters, making sure that the hot water is working and that the air conditioner is set properly, she disappears. It suddenly feels very odd to her to have brought two lodgers into her house. She had dreamt that they would enter it as if they were going back to their own homes, yet both of them had only one desire, to shut themselves away in their rooms without even looking at the house. Life with her lodgers will not be what she had dreamt of. She thinks about her accident again. Ever since she left the hospital, she has tried to think only of her night job at the Eden Palace and the money she made in order to have the Gold House restored. But now that she has finally rented both rooms, once again what she wants is for the truth to come out. Since her accident was a premeditated attempt on her life, she would have to discover who was behind it and file a complaint against him. It might be fate that she had rented one of her rooms to the deputy of Commander Roney Burke.

Once he has moved into his room, Willy Bost takes his notebook and pen from the inside pocket of his jacket.

On the second page, in the top left corner, he notes the date and time of his arrival at the Gold House. Below, in large characters, he writes: *Lizzie Malik, former acrobat of the Fuch Circus.* He underlines it twice, as if he were trying to make certain of something. He skips a line. *In the same house as Cassy Mac Key, whose coupe towed the Pontiac on the highway this very morning. Who is Cassy Mac Key?* He skips another line and underlines again: *The Gold House, a house for sleeping in. Beware of my old passion for the circus. Only one thing matters, what I came to San Rosa to do. What did I come here to do?* Then he turns the page, and writes in large letters: *Concentrate on that question alone.*

He is soaking wet despite the air conditioner, and his entire body is trembling. He takes a cold shower to help him get hold of himself. He changes suits. He always needs to wear clean clothes, especially in this heat, and he needs a clean body as well. He picks up his notebook and pen again, and, on the right-hand page this time, writes: *Stay calm. Above all stay calm.* He looks at himself in the mirror. His expression is placid. He regains confidence. It really was a good idea to buy that notebook before leaving. He will have to make sure he always has it with him, along with the pen, in easy reach. Write everything down right away, as soon as he feels the need. What would he do without his notebook? Even though he looks at himself in the mirror again and notices that his expression is as placid as ever, he feels more and more agitated, even overexcited. But by what? By his arrival in San Rosa? By Commander Roney Burke? By the Gold House?

If he were not afraid of causing complications on the first day of his stay, he would already have called Lizzie Malik to come and suck him in the darkness. He closes the shutters because he cannot bear the sight of the patio. He cannot bear to have the shutters open when he has a hard-on. His hard-on won't go away. He has to do something about it. Why does he suddenly want her to suck him until he ejaculates in her mouth without touching her, above all without touching her? But if he called her, how would she react? After all, she was once a circus performer, and everyone knows about the morals of circus performers! If she welcomed him just now in such a friendly way – a really excessive friendliness for the first day, he noticed it right away, in fact that was why he immediately began acting cold – it must be because she wants something. A hysterical doll, obviously, like all circus performers! Willy Bost paces back and forth in his room. The idea of continuing to jerk off all alone is intolerable. In the state he is in, he will never make it to ejaculation. And his hard-on will not go away until he takes enough sleeping pills to collapse into sleep. No, he did not rent a room at the Gold House just to jerk off all alone with no hope of ejaculation! That is out of the question.

He gets up, puts on his jacket, and walks toward the kitchen. Lizzie Malik is busying herself there. He asks her to come to his room on the pretext that the air conditioner has suddenly stopped working. When she comes in, she is astonished to see that he has closed the shutters. When, in the same expressionless voice he used to introduce himself a little earlier, he asks her to suck him, as if it were an order, it never occurs to her that he might be a maniac or a madman, of which there are a great many in the city center. She kneels down before him, and sucks him until he ejaculates in her mouth, crying out, without touching her, she notices that. She is not certain what she should do next, everything that has just happened was so unpredictable. He thanks her in the same expressionless voice and tells her that she can leave now. She could throw him out. She doesn't. As she is leaving, she tells herself that she will have plenty of time to think about what just happened between her and her lodger. The first day is not a day like any other. She tells herself that in order to keep her confidence up.

§6

It was completely by chance that Cassy Mac Key rented a room at the Gold House. When she left Willy Bost in front of the office of Commander Roney Burke, she wanted to go to the Babylon right away and introduce herself. She would never have thought she would be singing on a remodeled cruise ship whose engines had been removed so that it could never sail again. But the Babylon does not open until seven o'clock, and until then the gangplanks are raised so that no one can go aboard.

Not knowing what to do in this unfamiliar city, she goes and has a drink at the bar of the Eden Palace, just across from the Babylon. As she is reading the advertisements posted in the lobby, she comes across the one for the Gold House. The Babylon is reflected in the bar's mirrors. She finds the bay even more beautiful than the guidebook says, with its coral reefs off in the distance, and directly in front of her the lighthouse, looking like the tower of a sunken castle. The fishing boats from Gobbs's fleet have all left the docks. In their midst, the *Moby Dick* seems to be the king of the bay.

The *Moby Dick* is a copy of an old three-master that, according to legend, arrived four centuries ago in San Rosa. It was the first three-master to cross the reef and to enter San Rosa Bay. But the entire crew was dying of the plague. Only the captain, lashed to the wheel with a rope so as not to collapse from exhaustion, was miraculously uninfected. To prevent the *Moby Dick* from infecting the entire city, the governor decided to burn it in the middle of the night, with no warning. The captain perished in the fire. The day waiter at the Eden Palace recounts the legend to Cassy Mac Key, just as he does to everyone when they have a drink in the bar for the first time. When Cassy

Mac Key tells him that she is going to sing at the Babylon, he turns his back on her. At the Eden Palace, it is better not to talk about the Babylon.

Before going to the Gold House, Cassy Mac Key walks along the beach to look at San Rosa as if she were arriving by sea. That is when she discovers the volcano, its white peak overlooking the bay. She would never have thought it would be so close. It is as if San Rosa were huddled against the volcano to protect itself from the sea. Who would think, seeing it so peaceful, that it is only sleeping? What amazes her is the absence of a seafront, which gives San Rosa its unique character. She admires the brightly painted houses. There are no old houses because the volcano has already destroyed the city several times, all except Santa Cruce Church, with its two tall, asymmetrical towers.

It has been a long time since she has walked along a beach this way. She takes off her shoes so she can feel the sand burning her skin. She stretches out on the sand and closes her eyes. Old images come back to her before she can chase them away. She jumps up and runs to the ocean. A wave more forceful than she had expected knocks her over. Her dress is soaked and she is reeling from the violence of the blow. Because of the nearby reefs, the ocean is very dangerous in San Rosa. The waves are so powerful that they can knock you over in a moment and carry you out to sea, on deep currents that are impossible to resist. That is why swimming is forbidden.

What happened on the beach might explain why she had no desire to make conversation when she went to the Gold House. But she is also irritated by Lizzie Malik's excessive kindness. She tried to show Cassy Mac Key around the house as if she were a guest of honor. This welcome makes her uncomfortable, and her only desire is to find herself alone in her room. She invents a migraine caused by the trip. If it were not for the outside door giving onto the street, she would never have rented the room, despite the comfort of the Gold House. She cannot bear human contact when it becomes too insistent and too overbearing.

When Willy Bost arrives, she recognizes him right away from his expressionless voice, which resonates throughout the house like a gong. To her, Willy Bost is now the man whose expressionless voice resonates like a gong throughout Lizzie Malik's Gold House. But he is also – what a strange coincidence – the man with the Pontiac which she towed with her coupe this very morning on the highway to San Rosa. Willy Bost has hardly settled into his room before she is unpleasantly surprised to find that, while the Gold House has been restored with a great deal of taste, it has not been soundproofed. She hears everything happening between Willy Bost and Lizzie

Malik, and Willy Bost's cries growing louder and louder as he is sucked by Lizzie Malik. She could always plug her ears to keep herself from hearing. But on the contrary, she cannot prevent herself from clinging to the wall as if she wanted to embrace it. Willy Bost's violent orgasm as he is sucked by Lizzie Malik awakens her desire. She takes off her underwear so that she will be more comfortable. Clinging to the wall, listening to Willy Bost's spasms, she brings herself to orgasm again and again. But just afterwards, she weeps with rage. No matter how she tries to chase away the old images, she still has the same body, and therefore still the same atavisms. That is what she repeats to herself: the same atavisms. It is part of the inevitability she must live with. Is Willy Bost to be the new face of the inevitable for her? Their meeting this morning on the highway to San Rosa, and now their adjoining rooms in the Gold House, might suggest that he is.

She takes a bath to forget what has just happened and to help her think only about the Babylon. She puts on her pearl-gray raw silk suit to go and meet Dora Atter. On the lapel of the jacket is her jade brooch, the only one of her mother's jewels that she kept. The brooch, very old and of unknown origin, is a sort of talisman for her. She did not send her CV when she answered the Babylon's advertisement, because she knew from the beginning that with her CV she had no chance of being hired. She sent only a cassette with her latest songs, stating very clearly on the label glued to the cassette that she is the singer. She wrote all the songs recorded on the cassette during the dark years that she has just spent in a prison cell. Those are the only songs she wants to sing at the Babylon. To her great surprise, she was hired immediately. That was when she sold her mother's jewels, all except the jade brooch. The jewels are all she inherited from her mother, along with her voice. With the money from the jewels, she bought the beautiful old-fashioned coupe that she had admired in an auctioneer's window. She wanted to arrive in San Rosa driving that coupe. Now that she knows how pleasant it is to drive, she is not sorry to have bought it even though she knows it was a reckless decision. She is proud of her coupe. She can go wherever she wants and can even tow a Pontiac. Next Sunday she is planning to take it up to the volcano, which appeals to her as much as the bay.

§7

Willy Bost would surely be even more troubled by what happened between him and Lizzie Malik if he knew that in the room next door, clinging to the wall, Cassy Mac Key had brought herself to orgasm as she listened to his moans. Far from feeling relaxed, he feels terribly agitated again. This time his agitation is not accompanied by any excitement. In fact, it is exactly the opposite: a fevered agitation atop a central collapse, that is the condition he is in. He takes a second cold shower, shaves, and puts on his favorite aftershave. He does not want to put on the suit he was wearing just now when Lizzie came and sucked him. He chooses the light gray silk suit with a blue shirt and a fuchsia tie. He smiles at himself in the mirror. It is only when he steps away from the mirror that he begins to feel agitated again, to feel uncertain of who he is, to feel terrified, but of what? He puts his notebook and his pen into the inside pocket of his new jacket. He thinks about the Pontiac being repaired at the Grand Garage. He is anxious to see it running again. He is more and more eager to start work. This job as a deputy is the unknown, and the unknown is what he is looking for.

He takes the notebook out of his pocket and opens it to the second page. There is still a great deal of blank space on the page. What matters first of all is to cover all the blank space with ink. He writes: *Lizzie Malik, treated her like a professional, without paying her like a professional. Had she taken herself for a professional, then goodbye pleasure.* He adds: *The Gold House, a house for sleeping in where one can take one's pleasure as in a bordello, but without the inconveniences of a bordello.* He rereads what he has written, crosses out the period, replaces it with a question mark. Then he writes: *No mistakes. Above all no mistakes. That could be fatal.* He underlines *fatal*, puts the notebook back into the inside pocket of his jacket, smiles with a satisfied look. He has found his self-assurance again. The danger has passed. He can go out.

For his first night in San Rosa, he can choose between the Eden Palace and the Babylon. The idea of meeting Lizzie Malik working as a night waitress at the Eden Palace dampens his desire to make the acquaintance of Rosa Dore. He decides on the Babylon, despite his apprehension about hearing Cassy Mac Key sing. A few minutes are enough for him to see the condition of the city center. The old train station is completely dilapidated. The railroad tracks that still run through the center of town have become a crossroads for all sorts of illicit deals. There are rusty for-sale signs on the facades of all the hotels. Convertibles cruise back and forth looking for customers. The prices are posted above the dashboard. Willy Bost walks quickly, looking sure of himself. He is not afraid. He has fallen back into the habits of his profession. But why would anyone restore the Gold House in such a devastated neighborhood? That is a mystery, maybe the mystery of Lizzie Malik. His notebook is close at hand. He immediately takes it out and writes: *Do not try to uncover the mystery of the Gold House.*

Putting his notebook back into the inside pocket of his jacket, he thinks that he must look like a novelist taking notes for his next novel. That idea pleases him. But there is no question of his becoming a novelist even if he enjoys looking like one. He takes out his notebook again and adds: *Don't try to be what you are not. Be what you must be.* He has already covered a lot of blank space. It is easier than he would have thought to keep a notebook. He takes it out again and writes: *What matters is not that it be easy, but that it be useful.* He underlines *useful.* He does not have time to visit Santa Cruce. There is a crowd in front of the door. A young boy gives him a free invitation to the organ concert. On the card it says that Father Anders will make a special appearance in the pulpit after the concert. The title of his sermon is written in large letters: "Wake Up, Brothers, Wake Up!" Willy Bost shrugs his shoulders and throws the card into the gutter. He hates organ concerts.

Willy Bost is as surprised as Cassy Mac Key was when he sees the Babylon anchored in front of the Eden Palace. Buses with Santa Flor license plates are squeezed together in the large parking lot. They come across the border every day, taking customers on specialized tours to Gobbs's Amusement Park and then to the Babylon in the evening. Those buses are San Rosa's fortune. A hostess hands him a folder with a map of the Babylon and a list of all the services offered. Willy Bost takes his professional identification card out of his wallet. The hostess examines it with great care to make sure that it is not a forgery, then gives him a pass. With the pass, he can go everywhere for free, except to the special cabins.

Willy Bost will never forget Cassy Mac Key's entry onto the stage of the Babylon. She is wearing a very simple dress, with no collar and no jewels. Her hair is pulled back. She does not seem to be wearing any makeup. He hardly recognizes her. Without her pumps, wearing flats, she seems very small. She accompanies herself on the banjo as she sings, in an odd voice, determined and a little shaky. She sings with her eyes almost closed, detached, without gesturing. It is not the kind of show one expects to see at the Babylon. The words of her songs are very simple. They are about the bombs that never stop falling on Alejo, women from faraway places being sold from one whorehouse to the next up and down the west coast, a little girl crying in the falling snow because her dog has died, an old man freezing to death under a bridge as he watches a fireworks display lighting up the city, a woman who looks for love without ever finding it and finally gives birth all alone on a desert island, a poet who kills God as if he were His executioner, a priest somewhere in the middle of a desert who gives food to a dead man without noticing that he is dead.

The applause is so loud that Cassy Mac Key has to come back for several curtain calls. Her Babylon premiere is a success. Willy Bost does not go to pay his compliments in her dressing room. He is the first to leave the auditorium. He heads directly for the floor where the special cabins are. He pays for the works. He returns to the Gold House in a taxi. He sets his alarm clock for six. At eight o'clock he must be at the office, ready to start work.

§8

At the Eden Palace, this is not a night like any other. Tony Landry has finally announced his arrival, and he has reserved suite 103. Suite 103 is not just any suite. It is the one in which the big scene in *Eden Palace* was filmed. From the moment that Rosa Dore writes Tony Landry's name and the date of his arrival in her register, she is not the same. The Eden Palace can no longer be her entire life. It can no longer be her life at all, now that the Babylon has defeated it. It doesn't do any good to go from table to table singing her *Eden Palace* song, her charm is no longer enough to retain the customers.

Tonight, at last, Rosa Dore decides to have done with a situation that cannot be allowed to continue. She sends a telex to President Hardley to inform him that suite 103 has just been reserved by Tony Landry, and that he can no longer use it whenever he likes. How could she have accepted President Hardley's conditions, on the pretext that it was the only way to avoid bankruptcy? She also decides to break up with Commander Roney Burke. She cannot bear his increasingly wild passion. He can think of only one thing to do with her now, to throw her down on the big bed in suite 103 and make her come like, he says, no man will ever make her come. How could she have gone on so long pretending to be satisfied by Commander Roney Burke's sexual prowess, to the point of becoming a slave? How could she have lived all this time forgetting the pleasure that she had felt only once, in suite 103 of the Eden Palace, when she played the first role of her life?

Rosa Dore also decides that it is finally time to give in to Gobbs's advances. At midnight she will close the bar, and after having broken up with Commander Roney Burke, she will board the *Moby Dick*. Now she has a plan, to become the star of Tony Landry's new blockbuster. On her own, she will never be able to convince Tony Landry, who only makes movies with the stars of the Lossfell Company. What better mediator could she find than Gobbs to help her deal with Tony Landry? If Rosa Dore has not yet given in to Gobbs's advances, it is because she has never seen what might come of their relationship. With the arrival of Tony Landry, she finally sees what could come of it, and she can accept the idea of boarding the *Moby Dick*.

There is a terrible scene at midnight between Rosa Dore and Commander Roney Burke, particularly terrible because there is no explosion. He pales and trembles as he listens to her. He understands that it is useless to try to hold her back. Her decision is irrevocable. If he feels this wild passion for her, it is because she has always eluded him, and he has never been able to release her from the one role she played in suite 103 of the Eden Palace. When she has finished speaking, he answers that he will take her decision into account and act accordingly. He accepts her decision so easily because he has just made one of his own. That was how they left one another.

Lizzie Malik is relieved to learn of Rosa Dore's decision to close the bar of the Eden Palace. That way, she won't have to hand in her resignation. Leaving the Eden Palace to go back to the Gold House, she is surprised to see Nino waiting for her with a conspiratorial air. Nino is the dwarf of the Fuch Circus. He has always had a gift for playing roles, so why not that of the conspirator? When the Fuch Circus became part of Gobbs's Amusement Park, Nino became first the manager, then the director of the circus. He has come to meet Lizzie Malik in order to take her as quickly as possible to Nina's trailer. Nina is the giantess of the Fuch Circus. She has had a serious attack, and she asked Nino to bring Lizzie Malik without telling anyone. Lizzie follows Nino and thinks that today really is not a day like any other. If Nina asked to see her just after her attack, it might be because she wants to reveal something to her. Lizzie's heart is beating very hard, even harder than it used to every night as she climbed to the top of the rope to perform her act, defying death in order to get close to Livio.

§9

Cassy Mac Key wants to run away as soon as she boards the Babylon by the performers' gangplank. How can she sing her songs in a place like the Babylon? Maybe they hired her by mistake and are about to tell her. But where will she go then? She has nowhere to go. She would rather sing at the Babylon than leave for nowhere in her coupe.

Dora Atter is waiting for Cassy Mac Key in her office. No, there was no mistake. It was she, Dora Atter, the owner of the Babylon, who personally received Cassy Mac Key's cassette and who, after hearing it, immediately decided to hire her. Dora Atter is in the shadows, her eyes hidden behind dark glasses. She cannot bear light since her accident, which left her paralyzed. It is a miracle that she made it out of her burning car alive. She wears a black band around her hair. Her hair is so shiny that it seems to be made of jet. Now she will spend her life in her wheelchair, between her office in the Babylon and the *Salve Regina*, her new yacht, which she has made her home. Her hands are gloved in black silk. A little behind her, completely in the shadows, stands a dwarf with eyes like blue porcelain. She is Cidie, her companion. Cidie is mute. Cassy Mac Key cannot help wondering if that is really true, or if she is only mute when ordered to be, when there is someone in the office.

Next, Dora Atter talks to Cassy Mac Key about her songs. Her songs say everything one needs to hear and everything everyone must hear. That is why she hired her at the Babylon. She hopes that Cassy Mac Key will be happy singing there and that she will make everyone who hears her happy. Since Dora Atter says nothing about her salary or her contract, Cassy does not dare bring it up for fear of seeming ungrateful. Now Dora Atter has a favor to ask. Everything that goes on at the Babylon is transmitted to her by video in her office. But she does not want to see Cassy Mac Key's show only on video. She wants Cassy to sing for her before she sings on the Babylon's stage. She asks Cidie to leave. She wants to be alone with Cassy Mac Key to listen to her sing.

Cassy undresses. She puts on the little black dress she wears on stage and does her makeup and her hair. And then she sings for Dora Atter. She is taking off her black dress when Dora Atter asks her to stay that way for a moment, with nothing on. Dora Atter comes nearer and nearer Cassy Mac Key until she is pressed up against her. So it wasn't only for her songs that she was hired! Dora Atter runs her silk-gloved hands over Cassy Mac Key's body. Then she pinches her until bruises appear. She takes an instrument out of her pocket, and thrusts it into her vagina until she groans in pain. The instrument, too large, causes Cassy Mac Key to bleed. When she sees the blood, Dora Atter stops. She calls Cidie back in and asks her to take Cassy Mac Key to her dressing room.

As she is acknowledging the applause after having sung on the stage of the Babylon for the first time, Cassy Mac Key thinks of the price she has paid in order to be able to sing. She hopes that Willy Bost is in the audience, and that he liked her songs. When there is a knock on the door of her dressing room a few moments later, she thinks that it is Willy Bost coming to say hello and to invite her to dinner. But it is not Willy Bost, it is President Hardley. From the way he is dressed, with his round glasses and his bank clerk's suit, she would never have thought that she had before her the governor of San Rosa. He introduces himself with a humble and unassuming air. He is overwhelmed by her songs and does not know how to express his emotion. He invites her to dinner so that they can get to know each other. Cassy Mac Key cannot turn down President Hardley's invitation.

When she joins him in the cabin that is specially reserved for him, he is no longer the same man. He is wearing a white tuxedo and has taken off his glasses. He is slumped on a sofa, a glass of bourbon in his hand. The video screens set up facing the sofa show everything that goes on in the special cabins. On one of the screens is Willy Bost getting the works. President Hardley has rings on all his fingers, and he is perfumed like a woman. He watches Cassy Mac Key eat but does not touch any of the food himself. He cannot eat in the presence of a lady because he finds it indecent. He believes that a lady should be honored in every way. He believes that Cassy Mac Key is a lady, and he wants to give her the honors that are due to every lady. She is not hungry, but she forces herself to eat. She cannot prevent herself from looking at the video screen where Willy Bost is appearing in closeup.

President Hardley wants to know everything about Cassy Mac Key and he asks her to tell him everything. She answers that she has nothing to tell him because there is nothing to know. Then he says that she is not a lady and that he will prove it to her. He orders her to undress. Without any hesitation, he unzips his pants. Seeing the bruises on Cassy Mac Key's body gives him a hard-on. Dora Atter must have made them so that President Hardley would get a hard-on when he saw them. At the same moment, on one of the video screens, Dora Atter must be watching what is going on between President Hardley and Cassy Mac Key, just as President Hardley must have seen everything that happened between her and Dora Atter a little while ago, and just as she was now seeing everything Willy Bost is doing in his special cabin. President Hardley took an instrument out of his pocket, the same one Dora Atter had. They must buy them in bulk from the same shop. But unlike Dora Atter, it is not Cassy Mac Key's vagina that interests President Hardley. After having made her cry out in pain, he ejaculates, without having to touch himself or her. Then he asks her to get dressed. And he accompanies her to the parking lot like a gentleman. He smiles strangely when he sees her coupe. He tells her goodbye and good night as if she were a lady.

Willy Bost has just gone to sleep when Cassy Mac Key finally returns to the Gold House. She cries for a long time, as she did after her mother died. She could pack her suitcase and flee. But to go where? With her CV, no one would hire her. She has just come to understand this evening what it means to have been hired only on the strength of her cassette, without being asked for her CV.

§10

Nino brought one of the big trucks from Gobbs's Amusement Park to pick up Lizzie Malik. He is an odd sight, so small, sitting up very straight on the seat, his hands clutching the wheel, his head almost resting against the windshield. A thick cushion on the seat makes him taller. Lizzie sees how much he has changed. His hair has almost all fallen out. His face, once so merry, now expresses only his pride at being the director of the new Fuch Circus. He is silent. Lizzie does not try to break the silence. She does not forget that, like the others, he came to see her at the hospital and turned away from her when she told him about the cut made in the rope. Only Nina did not come, because her strength was giving out and she never left her trailer anymore. She has since made a change to fortune-telling. Her predictions are real oracles, and her trailer is the most popular attraction of Gobbs's Park.

Lizzie still remembers the emotion she felt each time she saw Nino and Nina's act. Nina sang in a thin voice while

Nino accompanied her on his string bass. The audience always exploded with laughter at first, as if it were a clown act. And then little by little it grew quiet under the tent, and the crowd listened, rapt, to Nina's voice and Nino's music. Nina's songs were in an unknown language. And yet it was as if everyone understood them. To Lizzie, Nina and Nino were the greatest artists of the Fuch Circus. Each time she saw their act it gave her the courage to go on with hers. She almost always thought she would never manage to do it again. She lived in constant fear of letting go of the rope and throwing herself into the void some day. The reason she had been hired at the Fuch Circus, without being part of the circus family, is that Dora Atter, who should have been the acrobat, had given it up because of a lack of talent and a hatred of the circus. No one would ever have imagined that Lizzie would become, through work and will, one of the Fuch Circus' best acrobats. After her accident, everyone thought she had exceeded her strength and that's what destroyed her. The story of the cut in the rope was never mentioned again.

Lizzie Malik has not been back to the Fuch Circus since her accident. Seeing the blue tent with its gold stars, she is very moved. The Fuch Circus was once her life and her dream! And now the circus is part of Gobbs's Amusement Park! Nina is waiting for Lizzie in her trailer. Her hands rest on the sheet, an old sheet embroidered with her initials and those of the Fuch Circus. Nino left Lizzie as she entered the trailer. Nina did not ask him to be there during their meeting. Even though they are inseparable, they do not tell each other their secrets. Lizzie entered without a sound. Nina's white hair, carefully arranged by Nino, makes a sort of halo. The trailer is lit by candles. Nina signals Lizzie to come and sit next to her.

The reason Nina asked to see Lizzie is that she wants to tell her a story. It is not just any story, it is the story of Livio. Nina and Nino raised him as their son. They had found him in a bundle in front of their trailer one morning, and they had no idea where he came from. Nina, who could not have children, thought he was a gift from Heaven. She wanted to make Livio the greatest acrobat of the Fuch Circus. Nina would have liked to be an acrobat along with Nino, if she had not been a giantess and he a dwarf. But just looking at the rope made Livio shake like a leaf. Instead of facing it, he would lie down on the sand and cry. His only desire was to follow Dora Atter everywhere she went and to imitate her in every way, in hopes of pleasing her. Even though Dora Atter hated the circus, her beauty captivated every eye and made her many conquests. Trying to distract Livio, Nino taught him the magic tricks he invented at night to astonish Nina and make her forget that he was a dwarf and she a giantess. But when Livio realized that Lizzie Malik was becoming the acrobat that he should have been, whereas all he ever did was repeat Nino's tricks without even attracting Dora

Atter's attention, he withdrew into himself, consumed by dark thoughts. On the day of the accident, he discovered by chance who had tried to kill Lizzie Malik and why. But when he told Nina, he made her swear never to repeat his words. He stayed one more year at the Fuch Circus, the time it took Lizzie to recover. Then he left San Rosa and never made his whereabouts known, not even to Nina.

Livio's story ends there. Nina makes it clear to Lizzie that she will tell her nothing more. She does not want to betray her promise. But she wants to give Lizzie a present before she leaves. It is her very old notebook full of songs. No one knows to whom it belonged, nor even who wrote all those songs in that language no one knows. Nina gives Lizzie her notebook as a way of asking forgiveness for not having told her what she had promised Livio never to reveal. She wants the notebook to bring her luck, in memory of the Fuch Circus. On the first page, she wrote: *For Lizzie Malik, these songs of love and death.*

Lizzie returns to the Gold House on foot. She holds Nina's notebook against her heart. She is deeply troubled to have learned Livio's story and to know at last that he was the one who discovered who had tried to kill her. And he came to the hospital every day for a year and said nothing! She loved him without knowing anything about him except what he showed in the ring when he appeared in his magician's outfit, with his magic boxes and his beautiful smile. It is as if she had loved a dream. Only now does she understand that she had never been anything but a stranger to the circus. The reason all the performers turned away from her after her accident is that they were obeying the law of the circus, which forbids them to betray one of their own, no matter what he has done. Regardless of what Lizzie did to make them accept her, she was never one of them, even if they let her think she was.

Lizzie wonders who could have cut through her rope and why. If Livio had made Nina swear never to reveal anything, he must have had his reasons. Nina did not give Lizzie any clues to help her discover what those reasons could be. Lizzie is completely lost. What has become of Livio and where has he gone? The idea that she has finally rented her two rooms reassures her. Above all she must look after her lodgers and make them want to stay at the Gold House. It is also essential that what happened between her and Willy Bost never happen again. What matters most is to discover who tried to kill her, and then to file a complaint.

§11

Waking up in the Gold House on his first morning in San Rosa, after having shaved and taken a cold shower, Willy Bost feels ready for anything. Yesterday seems long ago, almost unreal. A new life is beginning for him with this new position. Before putting his notebook into the inside pocket of his jacket, he abruptly tears out the first few pages. How could he have been so careless as to let it turn into a diary? He walks to the office of Commander Roney Burke. It is a mild morning. The air is scented by the flowers in the gardens along the bay. If it were not for the sight of the city center, like an infected wound, San Rosa could be paradise.

Commander Roney Burke is waiting impatiently for his deputy. He has been up all night. After leaving Rosa Dore, he came back to the office and went down into the archives. For the first time, he looked through his predecessor's files. His attention was immediately drawn to all the notes concerning President Hardley. After the opening of the border, his predecessor's one obsession was monitoring President Hardley. He tracked his movements from day to day, with a maniacal attention to detail. He must have been looking for something, and might have found it in the end, otherwise why would he have been killed in the pissotiére at the Fuch Circus? Commander Roney Burke knows that his predecessor did not die of heart failure as the coroner had reported. He has decided to change his work methods. Starting this morning, no case will be closed. He is finally going to show Rosa Dore who he is. If she decided to end their affair the way she did, it is because she thinks he is nothing. How could his passion have led him to become nothing? If he had not looked through his predecessor's files, he would never have known that President Hardley came to the Eden Palace every day. What did he come there to do and why did Rosa Dore hide it from him? Who is Rosa Dore? To him, she is the singer in *Eden Palace*, who enchants men with her fatal song. He has never tried to find out who she really is.

When he sees Commander Roney Burke, Willy Bost understands that something extraordinary happened the night before. The commander welcomes him to the office. Then he gives him his orders for the day. The first thing to do is to inquire into the places frequented by President Hardley during the tenure of his predecessor. He asks his deputy to begin with the Fuch Circus. What can President Hardley be doing there every evening at ten o'clock? He also asks him to write up a report. From now on, he wants to do as his predecessor did, write everything down so that there will be some trace of what they discover. From this day forward, he no longer considers his predecessor's death a closed case. Willy Bost feels that a great responsibility has been conferred upon him. Finally he has been given a task worthy of him. If there is anything to discover about President Hardley, he will have to be the one who discovers it. He is going to show who he is, and take his revenge on those who sent him to San Rosa without regard for his wishes or his merit. He decides to begin his notebook again, starting today. He writes the date, and under the date: *Investigation of President Hardley.*

After the departure of Commander Roney Burke, Willy Bost stays in the office for a moment to take possession
of the place. From today onward, this is no longer the office of Commander Roney Burke. It is the office of Commander Roney Burke and his deputy Willy Bost. He puts away his thermos in the part of the cupboard that is reserved for him. This morning, in the kitchen of the Gold House, he made some very strong coffee, the way he likes it, and poured it into the thermos while it was boiling hot. Next to the thermos he puts his medicine box. He lives in fear that his dizzy spells will start up again, and he always needs to have his medication close at hand. Finally he puts away his toiletries. He always likes to be impeccable, freshly shaved, his hair well-combed, his teeth always clean, with a nice smell of toothpaste. Next he turns to his desk, removes his appointment book and his pen-box from his briefcase, and takes his time placing them on the desk. There are no photos on the desk, and it seems empty to him. He drinks a cup of steaming hot coffee to cheer himself up. What a coincidence that his landlady was once an acrobat at the Fuch Circus! Maybe she can help him with his investigation? What is essential in an investigation of this importance, one concerning the city's most prominent figure, is determining whom to question and how.

Willy Bost arrives at the Fuch Circus at a sad moment. Nina has just gone into a coma, and all the performers are crowded in front of her trailer waiting for news. Willy Bost can go where he likes without attracting anyone's attention. Under the tent, his curiosity is aroused by the 45 sound of sobbing. Goppy, the hunchback of the Fuch Circus, is hiding in a corner of the ring. He is crying not only because of Nina, but also because he is going to have to leave the circus forever. He has just received a letter telling him that he has been let go, signed Gobbs. Nina's end will bring about Nino's end. It was thanks to them that Goppy, who was always their protégé, kept his job as ring boy. Crippled by pain and stiffness, he is less and less able to carry out his tasks. He is so pitiful when he walks into the ring all hunched over that everyone jeers at him. No sooner has he learned of Nina's approaching death than Gobbs lets him go.

Willy Bost sits down next to Goppy. Goppy needs so much to talk that he forgets to ask Willy Bost who he is and what he is doing in the tent. To Goppy, Nina's approaching death means the end of a world and the beginning of terrible changes. Even though Gobbs bought up the circus and made it a part of his Amusement Park, as long as Nina is alive, thanks to her ability to see the future, Gobbs is not the master, no matter how it seems. With Nina dead, Nino loses all his power, and Gobbs will finally become the master of the circus. Goppy believes there is no hope for the performers of the Fuch Circus. Gobbs will let them all go, one after the other. Very matter-of-factly, Willy

Bost asks Goppy why President Hardley comes to the Fuch Circus every evening at ten o'clock. Goppy answers without hesitation. President Hardley meets with Nina so she can read his cards. Without Nina, President Hardley would never have been able to remain invincible for so long, surrounded as he is by enemies who want him dead so they can take his place. In her way, Nina rules not only over the Fuch Circus, but over San Rosa. To Goppy, Nina is a queen, the last queen. He begins to sob again. Willy Bost can go now. Goppy will not tell him anything more.

It is just noon. Willy Bost goes to the Gold House for lunch since meals are included in the price of the room. This is his chance to introduce himself to his landlady in another light, and to make her forget what happened the day before. Lizzie Malik is just finishing the morning dishes when Willy Bost comes into the kitchen. She is relieved that he is behaving toward her as though nothing had happened. That is the best solution for both of them. He tells her about his visit to the Fuch Circus and his meeting with Goppy. Without mentioning that he is investigating President Hardley, he asks her if she knows that he has his cards read by Nina every evening at ten o'clock. She is very surprised to hear it. It gives her confidence that Willy Bost is talking to her so spontaneously, and she tells him the story of her accident. Willy Bost grows pale as he listens to her and nearly faints. His dizzy spells are back. When he feels better, he apologizes for his weakness, blaming the heat, which he is not used to. In an odd voice, he tells her that he will help her find the guilty party. Lizzie Malik really is continually surprised at her lodger's behavior!

He has scarcely gone back to the office when the telephone rings. It's Drove Wrangler, the manager of the Grand Garage, telling him that the Pontiac will be ready at six o'clock. That is good news, it proves that everything is going in the right direction. The telephone rings a second time. A voice, deliberately distorted, tells him to be at the pissotière at the Fuch Circus that night at eight o'clock. No further information is offered. Willy Bost shrugs his shoulders. Anonymous phone calls are common in his line of work, but they have no value. Nevertheless, he automatically makes a note of the rendezvous in his appointment book. The atmosphere in the office is stifling despite the air conditioner. Willy Bost feels ill again, with a sensation of vertigo.

After taking two pills, he goes out for a breath of air. The heat is heavy and there is no air. Black clouds are forming above the volcano. He walks to the beach. The sea grows darker as the clouds approach San Rosa. His entire body is trembling. He walks quickly in order to shake off his fear. He has never spoken of his fear to anyone. He has been living with it ever since the day he discovered his grandfather hanging in the bathroom of the rest home where he was spending his final days. The fear always comes back and surprises him, even when he thinks it is gone forever. When he tries to discover what he is afraid of, it is like a black hole. He suddenly notices a seashell half buried in the sand. It is pure mother-of-pearl, in the shape of a heart. He picks it up. He will give it to Cassy Mac Key to thank her for having so kindly helped him out on the highway. His breathing has become normal again, and he feels calmer. It is time for him to go back to the office and write his report for Commander Roney Burke.

There are two messages waiting on the answering machine. The first is from Commander Roney Burke. He has been delayed overnight on the other side of the border, and asks the deputy not to wait for him. The second is an invitation to the party on the *Moby Dick*, beginning at ten o'clock. If Gobbs is inviting him on his second night in town, it is because he wants to appear to be the master of San Rosa, even if he is not the governor. Willy Bost takes two more pills in order to regain control of himself. He writes his report, then locks up the office. The first step toward bringing everything back to normal is to pick up the Pontiac at the Grand Garage.

§12

After leaving his deputy, Commander Roney Burke goes to the shooting range, as he does every morning. President Patter is already there practicing. The commander feels sure of himself. All the targets are set out before him, in order of increasing difficulty. His hands are not shaking. For the first time, without knowing how, he misses the last target, which no one except him has ever hit. For the first time, President Patter hits the last target. So from now on he is the best shot in San Rosa. Commander Roney Burke has just lost his reputation. President Patter looks at him triumphantly. He must have been waiting a long time for this moment. Only now does Commander Roney Burke understand that President Patter must be pursuing a goal that he has kept hidden so that no one would mistrust him. The time for him to act must finally have come. In San Rosa, when you are the best shot, nothing stands in your way. Commander Roney Burke was the best shot, but he never knew how to take advantage of it, except to conquer Rosa Dore. What good did that do him, since he has lost her? Now he is nothing. They can shoot him down like a dog. His last chance is his deputy. No one in San Rosa knows who he is yet. They won't shoot him down until they find out who Willy Bost is.

Passing by the Grand Garage, Commander Roney Burke wonders why President Hardley goes there every day, as his predecessor had noted. There must be things going on at the Grand Garage that he does not know about, and which have nothing to do with trafficking in stolen cars. How many times has he closed his eyes to the activities of Drove Wrangler, despite the complaints he received, because

Rosa Dore asked him to? Who could have made Rosa Dore do that if not President Hardley, who frequented both the Eden Palace and the Grand Garage? Commander Roney Burke trembles as he thinks of all he should have seen and did not see because his passion was blinding him.

Once he has passed the border, he takes the Santa Flor Marina Road. The road has recently been resurfaced. On the site of the old lagoon, now entirely drained, stands the newly built Santa Flor hotel complex. The marinas are in the middle of construction. A seafront is being built there. Despite the beauty of the site, none of the investors wanted to build a seafront in San Rosa, because of the volcano. So it is in Santa Flor that the investors are building the seafront San Rosa would have been so proud to have. In the old days, there was nothing to Santa Flor but the lagoon and the swampy, mosquito-infested coastline stretching off as far as the eye could see. There was nowhere more unhealthy or more desolate. That was probably why they chose this place to build the Camp, with its sinister memories. Commander Roney Burke discovers that no trace remains of it. Where the Camp used to be is now the golf course, the pride of Santa Flor.

Commander Roney Burke parks his car at the end of the jetty, where an old man is fishing. The commander sits down beside him and asks him if the fish are biting. The fisherman is deaf. The commander has to repeat his question several times, louder and louder. The fisherman finally answers no, the fish never bite anymore, only tiny sardines. And he begins to shout, as if he were speaking to someone invisible standing before him, that it is all Gobbs & Fuller's fault. The Gobbs & Fuller Company owns everything in Santa Flor. No one can do anything to stop them. They are omnipotent and in control of everything. The fish began to disappear when Gobbs & Fuller took over Santa Flor. Gobbs & Fuller? So on the other side of the border, President Hardley and Gobbs, who are enemies in San Rosa, joined together to found Gobbs & Fuller? And it is the guests of the great hotel complex who cross the border to enjoy themselves at Gobbs's Amusement Park and Dora Atter's Babylon. As if San Rosa and Santa Flor were two become one, and as if everything were mixed together there contrary to all appearances. The old fisherman has just caught a tiny sardine. Disgusted, he throws it back into the sea. The commander walks back to his car. What more could he learn than what the old fisherman has just told him? If enemies in San Rosa are allies in Santa Flor, then there is no more hope.

The commander takes the road that follows along the coast toward the south. He opens the glove compartment and takes out his flask of old bourbon, the best there is. He drinks until the pain from his ulcer becomes unbearable. Then he swallows three tranquillizers and closes the glove

compartment. Outside, it is a real furnace. The sky is
leaden. Everything is black over San Rosa. The commander parks his car behind an old trailer from the Dominguez
Circus. A little girl comes out of the trailer. She seems very
happy to see Commander Roney Burke. She is waiting
for the return of her grandfather, who leaves early in the
morning in his boat in order to earn money. When he
is tired of that, he will take her to the other side of the
ocean. He worked all his life at the Dominguez Circus.
Now that the circus has closed, he lives only for his
boat. The grandfather enrolled her in a correspondence
course. She is a very good student and gets nothing but
perfect grades. The commander asks her what she does
when she has finished her homework and her lessons.
She laughs and shows him her bicycle leaning up against
the trailer. The commander wonders how old she might
be. Maybe thirteen? She has curly red hair and a face
covered with freckles. She is wearing an orange cotton
minidress with a print of white starfish. She looks at her
watch. It is time for her to go to her appointment. What
appointment? asks the commander. She laughs and does
not answer. Watching her pedal away on her bicycle, he
feels very sad. He takes the road again in the direction of
Santa Flor.

It is time to go back to San Rosa. Commander Roney
Burke suddenly wants to remain alone on the other side
of the border, and to spend the night there for the first

time. He drives along the main highway until he sees a motel, where he rents a bungalow for the night. He lies drowsing on the bed for a long time, in a daze. Then he runs a bath and turns on the TV. The picture is snowy because of the storm that has just hit. Not knowing what else to do, he has a drink at the bar. A girl sits down beside him and asks him to buy her a drink. She could be his daughter. But he has no daughter, he has no son, he has no family, he has no one but his deputy. The girl tells him her price. He thinks why not, since the TV isn't working. She follows him to the bungalow. She has a tape player in her bag. She always needs music as she works. She undresses like a professional, washes, then lies down. Very sure of herself, she puts a rubber on him. And then she lets him do as he likes. He doesn't like rubbers. But with the girl lying there, eyes closed, listening to the music with an ecstatic look, he feels so much pleasure that he forgets the rubber. Why isn't love always this simple? Why does passion come along and spoil everything? He pays the girl and gives her a tip, for the music, he says with a smile. When she leaves, he falls asleep, thinking of nothing.

§13

The convertible the Grand Garage lent Willy Bost is parked in front of the Gold House. All four tires are flat. At the same time as Willy Bost, Cassy Mac Key drives up to park her coupe. She laughs to see that he is having car trouble again. Just as before, she kindly offers to drive him to the Grand Garage. That is the best solution for him. In the pocket of his jacket is the shell that he had picked up for her on the beach. He squeezes it in his hand, thrust deep into his pocket. But why does he find it impossible to give it to her as he had intended?

Cassy Mac Key does not know what Willy Bost's hand is doing inside his pocket and is unaware of the drama unfolding there. He couldn't stop himself from crushing the shell. He holds the broken pieces in his hand. She looks at him, smiling at the coincidence that has made her come to his rescue a second time. Since he remains silent, she asks him if he is pleased with his first day in San Rosa. Delighted at this diversion, he tells her about the beginning of his investigation. As she listens to him, Cassy Mac Key thinks of what she could tell him about President Hardley. But the words would get caught in her throat. What would he think of her if she confided in him? She would never be able to tell him that she has just been released from prison. What she went through on her first night at the Babylon is her great shame, as if fate were still pursuing her. She is apprehensive about what might happen the second night, and how she will react if she sees Dora Atter and President Hardley again. She is also very troubled by what she has learned from Willy Bost, although he doesn't know that. It makes her feel that he is very close to her, and at the same time it intimidates her.

Sitting in the coupe, Willy Bost looks at Cassy Mac Key. She is wearing a low-cut sky-blue dress printed with white birds. He thinks she looks like a bird, but which one? She must have gone to the beach, because she smells like suntan oil. He should tell her that he came and listened to her sing the night before at the Babylon and that he liked her songs. But he can't. No more than he could give her the shell he had picked up for her, which is now crushed at the bottom of his pocket. Wanting to say something, he asks her which beach she had been to. She is very happy to be able to tell him about Angel Cove, at the end of the bay, away from the currents, where it isn't dangerous to swim. There is a buvette run by Mattie, the former costume maker of the Fuch Circus. Cassy Mac Key invites Willy Bost to swim with her at Angel Cove when he has an afternoon free. She will introduce him to Mattie's wonderful crab cakes. She has just made Mattie's acquaintance and already feels a great deal of affection for her. Willy Bost does not answer. How can he make Cassy Mac Key understand that he did not come to San Rosa to go swimming with her at Angel Cove on Sunday afternoons? The only thing that counts for him is his investigation. He will go alone in the Pontiac to question Mattie, who must have useful information about the Fuch Circus. Cassy Mac Key is embarrassed by Willy Bost's silence. She had not expected that he would not respond to her invitation. She drops him off in front of the Grand Garage. He gets out of her coupe and thanks her with a distant air.

The Pontiac looks like new. Drove Wrangler suggests that Willy Bost try it out with him to make sure that everything was properly repaired. Willy Bost is on his guard. Something tells him to be careful of Drove Wrangler. When Drove Wrangler asks about his first day in San Rosa, he answers that it was a quiet day, just the kind he likes. When they are back in the Grand Garage, Willy Bost reminds Drove Wrangler that he will have to tow the convertible parked in front of the Gold House, because all four tires are flat. He thanks him for everything, and asks for his bill from Gina Koll, the cashier at the Grand Garage. Gina Koll, looking him straight in the eye, tells him that since there is not one else around he can take the opportunity to look over the repair shop, which has just been remodeled. If he likes, she will go back to San Rosa with him afterwards. He understands that she is making advances. He is in a hurry to get back to her. In the repair shop, he walks distractedly from one car to another. Everything seems normal. At the back, there are three trucks from the Fuch Circus. Suddenly he wants to see what is inside them. The trucks are full of large crates piled on top of each other, impossible to open because they are sealed.

It is time for Willy Bost to rejoin Gina Koll. She is waiting for him by the Pontiac, wearing fresh makeup and perfume. She asks him if he is satisfied with his inspection. The repair shop is furnished with the very best equipment and operates at maximum efficiency. As soon as he drives off, she squeezes herself against him. If he wants to have another look at the repair shop, he can come back any day at the same time. He has hardly pressed down on the accelerator, happy to find that the motor has never run so smoothly, before she puts her hand on his fly. He grows hard as he drives. She unbuttons his fly and begins to suck him. She sucks exactly the way he likes it. He finds the situation terribly exciting. When he gives in to his orgasm, it is a paroxysm. It makes him let go of the wheel. Fortunately the steering had been readjusted and the Pontiac continues straight ahead without swerving. Now Gina Koll is smoking a cigarette. She asks him to drop her off in front of Santa Cruce Church, not telling him where she lives. He is still so stunned by the pleasure she gave him that he can only tell her he will see her very soon.

It is almost eight o'clock. To forget what has just happened, Willy Bost will go and look around the pissotière at the Fuch Circus. He parks the Pontiac far away so as not to attract attention. The pissotière is not part of the Amusement Park. On the door, it says: *No entry.* You have to wonder what it is doing there. Ever since the circus became part of Gobbs's Park, the pissotière has had no reason to exist. Willy Bost hides behind a low wall. At exactly eight o'clock, Drove Wrangler enters the pissotière. Five minutes later, he comes out with a black leather attaché case.

Willy Bost decides to wait a little longer. Whoever it was Drove Wrangler met there will surely come out soon. Night has fallen. The Amusement Park closes at seven o'clock, when the Babylon opens. Then the Volcano area empties out. A half-hour goes by and no one leaves the pissotière. Willy Bost cannot wait any longer. He has to return to the Gold House and get ready for the party on the *Moby Dick*. After all, Drove Wrangler might very well have picked up the attaché case without anyone else present in the pissotière. Anything is possible. He must be especially careful not to forget that. He is no longer inexperienced. He decides that it is best not to enter the pissotière despite his curiosity. The fact that he went to a rendezvous arranged by an anonymous phone call is already enough to arouse suspicion. Now they know that he is on the trail of something. Willy Bost really needs to talk to Commander Roney Burke. But it is tonight of all nights that the commander decided to leave him alone in San Rosa.

Willy Bost enters his room by the outside door so he won't have to make conversation with his landlady. He presses his white tuxedo with his traveling iron, being very careful not to crease it. He looks very handsome in his white tuxedo. He smiles into the mirror as he puts on his bow tie, midnight blue with white polka dots. Just before he leaves, he writes a few sentences in his notebook, and underlines these final questions in red: *Why are there*

crates in the trucks from the Fuch Circus parked at the back
of the repair shop of the Grand Garage? What could be in the
attaché case that Drove Wrangler carried from the pissotière
at the Fuch Circus at 8:05? What is Gina Koll trying to
accomplish by acting like a professional?

A rowboat meets the guests of the *Moby Dick* at the pier by
the beach and carries them back and forth. Willy Bost does
not know anyone. He never smokes, but he is smoking
now, to give himself something to do. And to boost his
confidence, he tells himself that he is on night duty. The
upper deck of the *Moby Dick* is crammed with people.
Willy Bost can come and go as he pleases. No one pays
any attention to him. He is already on his third glass of
champagne when a hand taps him on the shoulder. It
is Gina Koll, wearing an exquisite violet satin dress. She
casually asks him to invite her to dance. He's sorry, but
he doesn't know how to dance. Brightly illuminated, the
Babylon is visible from the upper deck of the *Moby Dick*.
Cassy Mac Key must nearly have finished singing by now.
The sky is full of lightning, as if there were fireworks over
San Rosa. The storm that had been threatening ever since
the afternoon has finally hit.

The music has suddenly stopped. A man in a mauve silk
suit invites his guests to go downstairs to the salons, where
a surprise awaits them. This is Gobbs. Next to him is Rosa
Dore, in a lamé sheath. They leave the deck accompanied

by a bald man dressed in leather. He is Tony Landry. Gina Koll knows everyone, and everyone greets her from afar without approaching her. Gobbs laughs and speaks very loudly. It grows dark in the salons. Gobbs appears on the video screens. The film, shot by Tony Landry, covers Gobbs's life story from his grandfather's fishing boat to the *Moby Dick.* At the end of the film, Gobbs announces his decision to run for governor in the forthcoming elections. Everyone applauds very loudly. Tony Landry takes the floor. He tells how honored he was when Gobbs asked him to make the film about his life, which should stand as an example to all. And he announces the return to the screen of Rosa Dore, whom he has just chosen to be the star of his next film.

Willy Bost listens distractedly. He feels the perfumed body of Gina Koll against him. Just remembering the scene in the Pontiac is enough to make him hard. He wants her right away. He lets her know it. She asks him to follow her. She seems to know the *Moby Dick* very well. She shows him into cabin 03, which is open. He takes her on the floor, without undressing her, rumpling and tearing her dress. It has been so long since he last took a woman that way, without restraint. He is like a madman. When he has reached the limit of his pleasure, he gets up and leaves without a word. There must be a spare dress in the cupboards of cabin 03, otherwise she would never have let him tear her dress that way. He goes back up to the deck. The storm has passed. He takes deep breaths. Rosa Dore is leaning on the railing, alone, facing the sea. He does not really recognize her as the person who appeared a moment before between Gobbs and Tony Landry.

On the beach, next to the pier where the *Moby Dick*'s rowboat has dropped him off, Willy Bost sees a woman who seems to be sleeping on the wet sand. It's Cassy Mac Key. What is she doing sleeping on the sand after the storm? Why hasn't she gone back to the Gold House? Willy Bost approaches her, as if to join her. But suddenly he changes his mind and turns around. He walks quickly toward the Pontiac. The coupe is parked next to it.

Back in the Gold House, he takes a shower to wash away Gina Koll's perfume. He is not sleepy, and goes out again for a walk. His steps lead him to the pissotière at the Fuch Circus. At this hour, the neighborhood is completely deserted. This time he cannot resist entering the pissotière even though it is not allowed. There, his head thrust into the urinal, a knife in his back, is a dead man. It's President Hardley.

Willy Bost immediately goes to the office to warn the Palace Security Division. The next morning, the *Gazette* announces the assassination of President Hardley in the pissotière at the Fuch Circus. Willy Bost, who discovered the body, also makes the front page.

Like everyone else in San Rosa, Lizzie Malik learns from
Sunday morning's *Gazette* that President Hardley has been
assassinated. It was Dany Sapin's great idea to distribute a
free special edition on Sundays. That was how the *Gazette*
crushed all its rivals, none of which could compete with
it. The people of San Rosa take great pleasure in eating
their Sunday breakfast while commenting on the Sunday
column of Dany Sapin. Dany Sapin writes his column
every Sunday to compete with Father Anders, who every
Sunday at Santa Cruce draws in more and more followers
with his sermons, which are the talk of the town. So the
people of San Rosa begin their Sunday by reading Dany
Sapin's column, and then go to Santa Cruce to hear Father
Anders's sermon.

Lizzie Malik is proud to have as a lodger Commander
Roney Burke's deputy, who last night discovered President
Hardley in the pissotière at the Fuch Circus, assassinated,
with a knife in his back. Now no one in San Rosa will be
able to act as though Willy Bost did not exist, even if he has
just arrived. They will have to reckon with him. In his column, which he must have written hurriedly upon hearing
the news, Dany Sapin expresses his rage. The assassination
of President Hardley is a blow to San Rosa, the tragic proof
that no one is safe here anymore. The only solution is to
demolish the city center and to construct a new center, one
worthy of San Rosa. Dany Sapin expresses his hope that
Gobbs will soon announce his candidacy, which everyone

is awaiting impatiently. Gobbs must become the savior of San Rosa and the avenger of President Hardley. Dany Sapin also expresses his confidence in Commander Roney Burke, now in charge of the investigation, who has already proven himself and whom everyone in San Rosa holds in high esteem.

To Lizzie Malik, unlike Dany Sapin, the assassination of President Hardley is not a bad thing. She is quite aware of the way he used Rosa Dore at the same time as he was paying the debts of the Eden Palace, and of what he did in suite 103, where he indulges his habits. She cannot stop herself thinking that the investigation into the assassination of President Hardley and her own investigation are connected. It may not be by chance that President Hardley was killed in the pissotière at the Fuch Circus. What was he doing there on a Saturday night, when the Amusement Park is closed? It is astonishing that Dany Sapin neglected to ask that question in his column. The pissotière at the Fuch Circus has always had a bad reputation. When she worked in the circus, Lizzie always went out of her way to avoid walking near it. She used to wonder why the Palace Security Division did not order it closed. It was the rotten core of the circus! And now it is in that very pissotière that President Hardley was found assassinated!

That is what Lizzie is thinking when Cassy Mac Key comes into the kitchen. Her dress is rumpled and her hair full of sand. She seems to be lost. Lizzie is surprised that Cassy

Mac Key could have spent the night outdoors, but she doesn't ask any questions. She offers her a cup of coffee and a piece of almond coffee cake, her Sunday specialty. But Cassy Mac Key cannot eat after the night she has just gone through. She feels like throwing up and her head is spinning. When she found herself all alone in her dressing room after having sung at the Babylon for the second time, she broke down in tears. And yet, this second night, she saw neither Dora Atter nor President Hardley, and she was applauded as enthusiastically as the first night. To escape her tears, she went to the bar and drank until her head was spinning so badly that she couldn't drink anymore. She had sworn to herself never again to drink alone in a bar, but it was stronger than she was, she couldn't resist. When she came out of the Babylon, the storm had just passed. She was in no condition to drive her coupe. She walked toward the beach without even knowing what she was doing. All at once she fell, and passed out. It was daylight when she came to. She knows nothing of the assassination of President Hardley, which Lizzie excitedly tells her about. From her reaction, Lizzie guesses that Cassy must have been acquainted with President Hardley. That does not surprise her. There are many rumors in San Rosa about President Hardley and the Babylon. Cassy feels great joy at the idea that President Hardley has been assassinated. It erases the memory of the night she has just spent lying unconscious on San Rosa Beach, and the shame she feels about it. It is as if the killer had avenged her. Now she is in a hurry to get back to her room so she can take a bath and change. She forces herself to drink coffee and eat a piece of coffee cake to regain her strength. She reminds Lizzie Malik of a little girl who has run away and who cannot get over being back home again.

This Sunday has begun well for Lizzie Malik. Now she is curious to know what the sermon will be at Father Anders's eleven o'clock service. Like many of the inhabitants of the city center, she makes a habit of going to the service, not to pray to God, whom she doesn't believe in, but to listen to Father Anders's sermon. Santa Cruce is even more crowded than usual. Silence falls as soon as Father Anders climbs into the pulpit. Everyone holds their breath waiting for the first words. Father Anders's voice wells up, deep and menacing. "Shame be upon him who, because the wrath of God has fallen upon him, was killed in the pissotière at the Fuch Circus!" Father Anders believes that President Hardley's assassin was inspired by God, and that the knife which killed him is the knife of God. Father Anders speaks like a man possessed. His voice swells and resonates throughout the church. Now he turns his attention to Dany Sapin's column. If the city center has become the rotten core of San Rosa, it is the fault of President Hardley, who did all he could to poison it until it became fatally tainted. What must be done is not to destroy the city center, but to save it, in order to make of it the city of God. Such is the message of Father Anders. He finishes his sermon by announcing his candidacy for the position of governor. He does not want to be a man of God only in the house of God. He wants to be a man of God in the city of men in order to defend the word of God there. God visited him in the night as he slept and gave him this mission. He needs the support of all his flock because he senses great perils ahead. The entire flock must unite as if for a new crusade. Lizzie is overwhelmed by Father Anders's sermon. He is the first to publicly denounce President Hardley and to contradict Dany Sapin. Lizzie does not share his faith in God, but she shares his will to save the city center. That is why she has just decided to support his candidacy. She did not have the Gold House restored only to let it fall prey to a demolition crew. Not since before her accident has she been so happy as this Sunday, on which both rooms are rented and President Hardley has been assassinated, and on which she has made the decision to join up with Father Anders.

As she does every Sunday after going to hear Father Anders's sermon, Lizzie pays a visit to her grandmother at the Holy Savior Rest Home. She takes the tram, just as she does every Sunday. The tram runs by the pissotière of the Fuch Circus, hidden by a large crowd. It is the great attraction this Sunday. The last tram stop is very near the rest home. In front of it is an esplanade with a panoramic view over all of San Rosa Bay, with the old lighthouse in the distance, where the reefs begin. The *Moby Dick* is not in the bay. It must have put out to sea, like the *Salve Regina.*

Lizzie is astonished that her grandmother is not waiting for her at the door of the rest home. Ever since she moved to the home, her grandmother has never forgotten that it is Sunday and that Lizzie is coming to see her. Sister Cize has spotted Lizzie and is coming to meet her. Last night's storm caused considerable damage to the garden. The flowers are battered and lightning has struck the great cedar tree. Sister Cize looks mournfully at her garden. She will have to get to work on it today, taking out everything that is damaged and planting new flowers. Sister Cize tells Lizzie that her grandmother had an attack last night because of the storm. She gave her a shot and now the crisis has passed. But today, to be prudent, her grandmother must rest.

Sister Cize accompanies Lizzie to her grandmother's room. She wants to talk. She has just heard the rebroadcast of Father Anders's sermon on the radio, and she is still feeling emotional about it. If she had not taken a vow to spend the rest of her life looking after the Holy Savior Rest Home, she would have gone immediately to join Father Anders. She took her vow to avoid ending up like her sister, who was found dead one morning in her convertible. Lizzie's grandmother is very attached to Sister Cize, and Sister Cize adores her to the point of spoiling her more than any of the other lodgers. Every day, she brings her a bouquet from the garden so that her room will always smell of flowers. Sister Cize believes that Lizzie's grandmother has been blessed by God. Lizzie smiles at Sister Cize. To console her for not being able to join Father Anders, she tells her that, since she is lucky enough to live in paradise, she should never leave it. Sister Cize has a pure and simple soul. Outside the home, she would be lost.

Lizzie's grandmother rests in the shadows, her hummingbird at her side. She found it one day on the windowsill, its leg broken. She took care of it while it healed. She leaves the window open so that it can fly about the garden. But it always comes back. She talks to the hummingbird as if it understood everything. She calls it the philosopher. She has long discussions with it about the meaning of life and what awaits us after death. She says that she finally understands philosophy, even though she has never been to school and does not know how to read. Lizzie takes her grandmother's hand. They are so happy on Sunday when they are together. Lizzie tells her about the past week. She has many things to tell her today: the arrival of her two lodgers, the end of her night job at the Eden Palace, the assassination of President Hardley, Father Anders's sermon, and her decision to support his candidacy for governor of San Rosa, in order to defend the city center and to save the Gold House. Lizzie tells her grandmother everything. The only thing she never talks about is the Fuch Circus. Her grandmother thinks that the Fuch Circus was Lizzie's great unhappiness and her biggest mistake. She sacrificed everything in order to become a great acrobat, and she sacrificed everything for nothing because her accident put an end to her dreams. Lizzie has never told her grandmother that it was not an accident. What consoles Lizzie's grandmother is that Lizzie restored the Gold House after her accident. And now she wants to fight to defend the city center. So it was not in vain that the grandmother made sacrifices in buying the Gold House so that she could leave it to Lizzie as an inheritance.

When she has finished talking about her week, Lizzie notices that her grandmother has fallen asleep. She kisses her gently without awakening her and leaves the room on tiptoe. When she comes back to the Gold House, no one is there. She takes advantage of her lodgers' absence to give it a good cleaning. She dines alone and goes to bed early.

§15

Cassy Mac Key climbs out of the bathtub. The assassination of President Hardley has chased away her dark thoughts and erased the memory of the night she has just spent on the beach. She wants to take advantage of the peacefulness of Sunday and the beauty of San Rosa after the storm. She decides to have lunch with Mattie at Angel Cove. Afterward, she will head toward the volcano to see

what it looks like close up. She does her hair and makeup.
She chooses a blue dress with a sailor collar, and she takes
a white angora cardigan with her because it must be cold
at the top of the volcano. Her coupe awaits her in front
of the Gold House. As soon as she climbs in, she feels
light and sure of herself, as if nothing bad could happen
to her.

As she approaches Angel Cove, Cassy is surprised to see
smoke rising in the sky. The cove shines in the sun, and
the sea is the color of emeralds. The buvette is smoldering.
Mattie is nowhere to be seen. Cassy cannot believe that the
fire could have started by itself. She thinks of Mattie, for
whom she had felt an immediate friendship. They had
swum together. And then Mattie suggested she try her
crab cakes. She had opened a bottle of white wine, as if to
celebrate their meeting. They had drunk a little and their
heads were spinning. They had lain down on the sand to
sunbathe. Cassy had told herself that she might have a
friend she could talk with about her past, who would give
her advice so that it wouldn't all start up again like before.
Mattie did not tell her why she had left the Fuch Circus.
She only showed her the beautiful costumes she kept in a
trunk as if they were some kind of treasure. She also told
her about her plan to open a diving club. Down at the
bottom of Angel Cove there is a submerged grotto whose
wonders Mattie wanted to show her. Cassy told her that
every time she dives she is afraid the sea will swallow her

forever. Mattie laughed. They would dive together, and they would go to the grotto.

Cassy cannot stay any longer watching the buvette burn. She stops at the first phone booth she comes to and leaves a message for Willy Bost. There might be a connection between the assassination of President Hardley and the burning of Mattie's buvette. Cassy Mac Key is very happy to be useful to Willy Bost. The investigation of President Hardley concerns her personally. She goes back to the Gold House hoping that Lizzie Malik will still be there. Lizzie must have known Mattie, since they worked together at the Fuch Circus. Suddenly Cassy is anxious to question her so she can find out more about it. But there is no one at the Gold House. Cassy takes a piece of coffee cake and heads for the volcano.

The road stops halfway up. A trail continues on, but there is a sign at the entry to the trail that says *Motor vehicles prohibited.* Cassy acts as though she hadn't seen the sign. There is no danger on a Sunday. The trail is stony and rutted. She must be careful not to stall the car, or else she'll never be able to start up again. She remembers everything she learned in driving school, how important it is to push gently on the accelerator so as not to overburden the engine. A large buzzard flies above her, as if he were leading her. She takes deep breaths. Suddenly the air is almost cold. What a change from the stifling heat in San

Rosa! It makes her forget the fire at the buvette. She can already see the summit of the volcano, peaceful in the blue sky. The snow glints and dazzles her. The trail has become smoother. The coupe climbs effortlessly. She was right not to pay attention to the sign. She turns off the engine. Just in front of the coupe is a motorcycle. So she is not the only one who thought of going to the top of the volcano, even though it is forbidden.

Cassy runs to the volcano. Beneath her is the crater, like a bottomless black hole. It seems to be completely extinct. Cassy sits on the rim. She feels an exaltation at being there at the summit of the volcano, far from San Rosa. If anyone else is near, she doesn't see them. She eats the piece of coffee cake she brought with her. The cake is velvety, veined just as it should be, and wonderfully flavored. She would like another piece. She is very hungry all of a sudden because of the altitude. She lies down on the moss between two patches of snow. Here, atop the volcano, she forgets everything that is happening below. The buzzard glides above the crater, then dives.

Cassy has stayed like this an hour, immobile. A man with a camera on a strap is looking at her. He waves and comes to join her. He introduces himself right away: Stive Lenz. He has signed a contract with the Lossfell Company to make a movie about San Rosa, and he is living in the Eden Palace, where Lossfell has reserved a room for him. The first thing he wanted to see was the volcano. Cassy introduces herself in turn. She sings at the Babylon at night and she lives in the Gold House. Stive Lenz is very self-assured, quite the reverse of Willy Bost. He is very happy to share his passion for volcanoes. In his opinion, it won't be long before the volcano erupts. He hopes it will be a splendid eruption and that he will be able to film it. It was because of the volcano that he accepted the offer from Lossfell to make a movie about San Rosa. If he were not a cameraman, he would be a volcanologist. He looks at Cassy Mac Key as he speaks. She thinks that he knows how to charm and that he enjoys love. She finds him attractive, even if he is not for her. She knows that instinctively, just as she knows of her attraction to Willy Bost, which she cannot resist, even if it hurts her. She makes the most of the pleasure she feels at being in the company of Stive Lenz at the edge of the volcano. He accompanies her to her coupe, which he compliments her on. He will come and hear her sing at the Babylon soon, that is what he says as he is leaving. With his motorcycle, he very quickly speeds ahead of her, and disappears down the trail.

It is not yet night when she returns to San Rosa. She still has time to go back to Angel Cove before she has to sing at the Babylon. She hopes that Mattie will be back and will be able to explain what happened. There are only ashes and blackened boards where the buvette used to be. The cove looks desolate. Mattie is not there. Cassy finds the heat unbearable now that she has been to the volcano. She does not want to swim. The water seems treacherous in spite of its clarity. In the distance, she sees the *Moby Dick* coming back to San Rosa. She closes her eyes. Suddenly her body seems as heavy as lead.

§16

It is the customs officer at the border who, handing him the Sunday *Gazette*, informs Commander Roney Burke that President Hardley has been assassinated during the night. Anything can happen, thinks the commander, even when you think that nothing can ever happen again. He would never have thought it possible that President Hardley would be assassinated. To him, and to all the people of San Rosa, President Hardley was stronger than death. He had imposed his rule for so long, as if he were invincible. And now he has been killed in the pissotière at the Fuch Circus, where, as if by chance, his predecessor was killed. How strange it is that this coincides with the arrival of his deputy, and that it was his deputy who discovered the body! The commander finishes a flask of bourbon in one swig. The pain from his ulcer makes him cry out. To hell with the ulcer. He takes a double dose of tranquillizers. His heart is beating irregularly and he is covered with sweat.

Willy Bost has spent the rest of the night at the office. He is writing in his notebook when Commander Roney

Burke enters. With authority, the commander asks his deputy to give him a summary of everything that has happened. Willy Bost's summary is clear and precise. The commander congratulates him on his initiative and his logical way of putting facts together. He believes that those two qualities are essential for success in an investigation of this importance. In turn, he very briefly informs his deputy of what he has learned in Santa Flor. Even though it is Sunday, there is no question of their putting out to sea in the *Mangor*, as the commander had planned. The commander will make inquiries at the *Gazette* while Willy Bost asks Goppy some more questions.

So Willy Bost returns to the Fuch Circus. All the trailers are closed up. He knocks on the doors but no one answers. The circus performers must have agreed among themselves not to allow intruders. Willy Bost knocks on Nina and Nino's trailer. Since there is no answer and the door is not locked, he decides to enter. There are even more candles lighting up the trailer than there were the day before, and there are flowers everywhere. Nina is lying on her bed, dressed in her most beautiful costume. Next to her, also dressed in his most beautiful costume, is Nino, his hand in Nina's. Both seem to be sleeping. But they are dead. Nino did not want to outlive Nina.

Willy Bost goes back to the big top in hopes of seeing Goppy. The ring is illuminated, but empty. All of a sudden, raising his eyes, he sees an acrobat practicing at the top of the rope. Who could it be? There has not been an acrobat in the Fuch Circus since Lizzie Malik's accident. Willy Bost is careful to make no noise, in order to avoid being noticed. Watching the acrobat's performance, he thinks that it must be a tribute to Nino and Nina. The acrobat's gestures are stiff and even rather clumsy, but it is a captivating performance. At the end, the acrobat climbs down and bows to the empty tent. Willy Bost stands up and begins to applaud and to shout bravo. He has an image of himself as a child, next to his grandfather, applauding a couple of acrobats. Immediately afterward, he seems to have a black veil over his eyes. His dizziness has come back unexpectedly. His head is spinning so fast that he is forced to sit down.

The acrobat comes and joins him, curious to know who was applauding him, when he thought he was alone. He has a deep scar on his forehead. Willy Bost conquers his dizziness. He introduces himself so that the acrobat will introduce himself in turn. He is Livio, the former magician of the Fuch Circus, the adopted son of Nino and Nina. He answers Willy Bost's questions without hesitating, as if he wanted to clear his conscience. After having left San Rosa, he signed up with the Dominguez Circus of Santa Flor. He wanted to learn to become an acrobat at last, on his own, in order to carry out Nino and Nina's wishes. But he came back too late, when they were dead. Livio wants to tell Willy Bost everything he knows about Lizzie Malik's accident. He has finally found the courage to speak. It was Dora Atter who asked Goppy to cut the rope. She could not bear to see an acrobat triumph in the Fuch Circus, which she wanted to destroy. It was Goppy who told him that, just after the accident, when Livio caught him trying to hide the rope. Weeping, Goppy admitted it all to him. He had destroyed himself for Dora Atter, who was his goddess, even if he loved the Fuch Circus more than his own life. Livio asks Willy Bost not to prosecute Goppy. Even though he is guilty, he is not responsible. His simple mind could not resist the hold Dora Atter had over it. When he realized what he had done to Lizzie Malik, he tried to hang himself in his trailer with the same rope. It was Nina who saved him, and then looked after him, along with Nino. No one is more devoted to the Fuch Circus than Goppy. When Livio understood who Dora Atter was, he too, like Goppy, wanted to die. No one will ever know why Dora Atter wanted to destroy the Fuch Circus and its last acrobat. Livio thinks that it is her secret, as it is also the secret of the Fuch Circus, which she was the last to inherit.

Now Livio wants to go sit with Nino and Nina, and ask their forgiveness. His passion for Dora Atter was his greatest folly. Willy Bost returns to the office. Cassy Mac Key's message is on the answering machine. What could the burning of Mattie's buvette have to do with his investigation? The ideas jostle each other in his head. Now he will have to go to Angel Cove to see what really happened and to question Mattie. As he passes the Grand Garage, he cannot help but stop in. As on every Sunday, the Grand Garage is closed. But the emergency exit of the repair shop is open. Just as he is about to enter, he sees Drove Wrangler, with his black leather attaché case in his hand, walking toward a blue Chevrolet. The garage door had opened automatically. Willy Bost runs to his Pontiac. He is going to follow Drove Wrangler, even at the risk of being recognized.

Beyond the border, Drove Wrangler takes the Santa Flor Marina Road, then the lane that runs along the ocean. Since it is Sunday, there are many cars on the road, and Willy Bost is not noticed. Suddenly he sees Drove Wrangler park the Chevrolet in front of an old trailer from the Dominguez Circus. A little girl in a red dress is waiting for him by the door. Drove Wrangler disappears into the trailer with her. A few moments later, a boat draws up on the beach. Drove Wrangler runs toward the boat, from which an old man is waving to him. The little girl has closed the door of the trailer again. Off the coast is the *Moby Dick*, with all its sails unfurled. Willy Bost carefully writes down in his notebook what he has just seen, so that he can report it to Commander Roney Burke.

Night is already falling when he arrives at Angel Cove. He did not expect to see Cassy Mac Key's coupe. She has nothing new to tell him since she has not seen Mat- tie. Willy Bost walks the perimeter of Angel Cove but finds nothing. He leaves Cassy Mac Key very abruptly, without even taking time to ask her about her Sunday. He goes directly back to the office. On the answering machine is a message from Commander Roney Burke, asking him to meet him as soon as possible on board the *Mangor*.

§17

This same Sunday, arriving at the offices of the *Gazette* after leaving his deputy, Commander Roney Burke is unpleasantly surprised to discover that there is no one around. All the staff of the *Gazette* are on board the *Moby Dick* for a sea cruise. Gobbs isn't wasting any time. No sooner has President Hardley died than Gobbs begins his campaign. The *Gazette* is no doubt going to put out a special issue on him. Commander Roney Burke looks at his watch. It is time for him to go practice at the shooting range. Missing his practice would be out of the question. President Patter is not there. He has joined Dora Atter on board the *Salve Regina* for a sea cruise. To the commander, that confirms his hypothesis that President Patter has a plan, which he might be about to carry out, having made an alliance with Dora Atter. She is now the principal stockholder of the Fuller Bank.

Since everything seems to be happening at sea this Sunday, Commander Roney Burke has only to reboard the *Mangor* and put out to sea himself. He will stop and say hello to Mattie as well, as on every Sunday. He does not know what she does all week, just as he knows nothing about her past. When they are together, they talk about the sea and all the treasures it hides, which you have to discover if you want to know happiness. They drink white wine and eat crab cakes, and then they leave each other until the following Sunday. She never asks him about himself, as if she didn't dare.

Commander Roney Burke arrives at Angel Cove a little before Cassy Mac Key. So he is the first to discover the burning buvette. But behind the buvette he also discovers Mattie, dead of a bullet through the heart. He stands for a long time without reacting. Then he carries Mattie to the *Mangor*. He goes down into the hold and lays her out on the spare ropes. He realizes by the pain that he feels how attached he was to her. But he had never wanted to know anything about that either.

Mechanically, the commander puts out to sea again. He is already working on his second bottle of bourbon. The tranquillizers can do nothing to soothe his ulcer. From afar, the *Mangor* follows the *Moby Dick*, which is following the *Salve Regina*. With his binoculars, the commander can see the deck of the *Moby Dick*, where Rosa Dore is in animated conversation with Tony Landry, while Gobbs gives a press conference in front of the staff of the *Gazette*, who are drinking in his words as if they were receiving oracles. The pain he feels at Mattie's death prevents him from becoming enraged at the sight of Rosa Dore on board the *Moby Dick*.

The *Salve Regina* comes to a stop facing Santa Flor, soon followed by the *Moby Dick*, which pulls alongside. Commander Roney Burke sees Gobbs climbing aboard the *Salve Regina* to join Dora Atter and President Patter, who are awaiting him on deck. What they are saying to each other, neither Commander Roney Burke nor the staff of the *Gazette* can hear. Now that President Hardley is dead, Gobbs must be seeking a new alliance with the Fuller Bank. If Dora Atter has allied herself with President Patter, it can only be because, like him, she has a plan. Commander Roney Burke is feeling very ill. What he has just seen, the encounter in midocean of the *Moby Dick* and the *Salve Regina*, is the proof that his investigation will serve no purpose and will lead nowhere.

The commander lies down on the deck. He wants to let the *Mangor* drift out to sea in the direction of the reefs. The *Mangor* has already been out there once, piloted by Mattie's father, and it ended up shipwrecked. It was just afterward that Commander Roney Burke bought the *Mangor* from Mattie, who wanted to get rid of her father's boat. What did Mattie know that would make someone want to kill her? And what did her father know that made

him want to go and be shipwrecked in the middle of the reefs, when like all the fishermen in San Rosa he knew that it was death to approach them? The commander never tried to find out why Mattie had left the Fuch Circus, or why she lived alone at Angel Cove. She was still very attractive. Why did she not start her life over again? The commander has only one desire, to lie down alongside Mattie on the ropes at the bottom of the hold and let himself be carried away, along with the *Mangor*. It is the thought of his deputy that gives him the strength to resist his desire and return to San Rosa.

When Willy Bost boards the *Mangor* he thinks there is no one there. The cabin and the deck are deserted. It is only when he goes down into the hold that he finds the commander, lying on the ropes, holding Mattie in his arms. The commander is shaking all over and talking as if he were delirious. Willy Bost realizes that the woman the commander is holding in his arms is Mattie. He has a certificate in first aid. Quickly he goes and gets the medical kit from the cabin and gives the commander a shot. Then he carries him back up to the cabin and lays him down. Soothed by the injection, the commander falls asleep.

Willy Bost feels greatly distressed. He needs the commander to restore his courage. But he is the one who needed his deputy to stop him from slipping away as he wanted to. In the cabin of the *Mangor*, sitting next to the commander, who is lying on the bunk with his eyes closed, Willy Bost no longer believes in luck. What could the investigation lead to? Once again, he has exulted over nothing. He stays for a long time in this state of distress, while the commander rests beside him, calmed by his presence.

When the commander wakes up in the middle of the night, he asks his deputy to take Mattie to the Fuch Circus so they might pay their respects to her one last time, and so the circus performers would know how she had died. He also asks him, while he himself is recovering from his attack, to carry on the investigation alone, as if it had to lead somewhere. Then he tells him what he saw in the middle of the ocean. Willy Bost gives the commander a second shot to help him go back to sleep. And he leaves, promising to come back soon.

The lights are out in the trailers, and the circus seems deserted. Willy Bost turns on the lights in the big top. And he lays Mattie down in the center of the ring. She who has always lived away from the spotlight has earned the honor of being in the ring. Willy Bost watches over her so that she will not be there alone. Without knowing what he is doing, he embraces her and weeps. He squeezes her hard, as if he wanted to melt together with her. At daybreak, he goes back to the Gold House. He takes a pill so he can sleep for awhile without thinking about anything. Soon he will continue the investigation, as Commander Roney Burke had asked.

§18

For the first time, Lizzie Malik eats breakfast with her two lodgers. Cassy Mac Key has had a very bad night, what with her nightmares starting up again, and she woke up with a bad feeling about things. When Willy Bost tells her what happened to Mattie, she is not surprised to hear it. That was when Lizzie Malik told them about the affair between Mattie and Drove Wrangler, back when Mattie was a costume maker and Drove Wrangler was a regular at the Fuch Circus. From that time on, Mattie was a completely different person. She used to care about and listen to everyone, but she became withdrawn, never speaking to anyone anymore.

Willy Bost is thinking. If Drove Wrangler was a regular at the Fuch Circus, it was surely not only out of love for Mattie. Mattie might have been so blinded by her passion that she did not try to find out who Drove Wrangler was or what he was expecting from her. Willy Bost cannot stop himself from getting carried away with his investigation, even though he now knows that disentangling the threads will not make him any friends in High Places, and won't earn him the transfer he has been longing for. They will behave as if nothing had happened, as usual. Each time that he has been about to wrap up an investigation, they suddenly took him off the case, on the pretext that he had made a serious error and that his reasoning had gone awry. The official justification for his ranking, which was always at the very bottom of his category, was always the same: "Lack of logical thought. Impulsive and undisciplined mind. Mistakes his dreams for reality." Rather than try to untangle the threads in order to make an impression on those in High Places, he should be trying to untangle them for himself. He has to convince himself that San Rosa is his last chance.

Willy Bost is not about to waste time by accompanying Cassy Mac Key to the Fuch Circus, as she has just requested. When you are a singer at the Babylon, you can handle anything, he thinks. Now is not the time for him to forget his motto: don't get sentimental, don't ever get sentimental. The uncontrolled emotion that took hold of him as he was sitting up with Mattie must never happen again. Commander Roney Burke is an example not to follow. What a sad sight it was when he discovered him in the hold of the *Mangor*, lying on the ropes, embracing Mattie as if he could never let her go. Let that be a lesson to him! Lizzie Malik offers to accompany Cassy Mac Key to the Fuch Circus. They will go together and pay their last respects to Mattie. Willy Bost takes advantage of their conversation to disappear.

The first thing Willy Bost does when he is alone in his room is to write down in his notebook everything that
has happened since he went aboard the *Mangor*. It is no longer enough for him to investigate as he has always done. Now he needs a notebook to write down everything that happens. The threads become untangled as he writes. Willy Bost feels great pleasure in writing. His style is growing more sure. He is learning to master his style. But what has he been until now, if not the slave of those in High Places? The reason he came to San Rosa, and he trembles to think of it, might be finally to become the master, rather than remaining the slave who rebels because no one respects his merits and no one takes account of him. And he is becoming the master through this notebook, which he can no longer do without. What Commander Roney Burke saw on the open sea, the meeting of the *Moby Dick* and the *Salve Regina*, is the great lesson that he needed. The gangs can run wild and wage war on each other in San Rosa, but the leaders, on the open sea, meet to talk business and to prepare for the future. Until now, when he was carrying out an investigation, Willy Bost saw only what was happening on land, knowing nothing of the open sea. So how could he ever have brought an investigation to a close?

Willy Bost goes to see Commander Roney Burke. The commander is sitting on his bunk. His pulse is weak but regular. Willy Bost gives him another shot. The commander is stable. It is not his time to die. Since he was unable to love Mattie in life, what good does it do to join her in death? That would be even more mad than his mad passion for Rosa Dore. What has just happened to him is exactly the warning he needed. He decides to give up bourbon. He has not forgotten the shame he felt when for the first time he missed the last target, which he had always been the only one to hit, and when, to his even greater shame, President Patter hit it for the first time. When he goes back to the shooting range, it will be to erase his shame. He has not given up.

The commander asks Willy Bost to take the Santa Flor Marina Road to the old trailer from the Dominguez Circus, and to question the little girl. He has a theory, but he doesn't know how to prove it, that Drove Wrangler, even as he was dealing with Gobbs and the Fuch Circus, was working for President Hardley, whom he betrayed at the very end. So it might have been at his request that President Hardley went to the pissotière at the Fuch Circus where his enemies were waiting to kill him. The commander is more and more convinced, but he doesn't know how to prove this either, that it was Dora Atter and President Patter who had President Hardley killed, President Patter out of ambition and Dora Atter out of vengeance. Everyone in San Rosa is aware of her impossible passion for President Hardley. They needed Drove Wrangler to draw him into the trap where he would be killed. If Commander Roney

Burke's hypothesis is correct, Drove Wrangler will never be seen again. The commander is inclined to think that Mattie's murder has nothing to do with what is happening in San Rosa. Her death might be the tragic outcome of a cursed passion which she wanted to escape by taking refuge in Angel Cove, and which caught up with her.

Willy Bost follows Commander Roney Burke's orders. Passing by the Grand Garage, he cannot resist his desire to see Gina Koll again. If she was invited to the party on the *Moby Dick* and if she knows the ship so well, it must be because she sees a lot of Gobbs and spends a lot of time there. As long as he knows how to go about it, he will surely be able to get some valuable information out of her. Just seeing her sitting behind the cash register at the Grand Garage is enough to give him a hard-on. Gina Koll waves to him. It is time for her break. Why don't they go for a drive in the Pontiac? He thanks her for her offer, but he doesn't have time because of an urgent appointment on the other side of the border. Laughing, she tells him to stop by on his way back.

He gets back on the road he took the other day as he was following Drove Wrangler's Chevrolet. The Chevrolet is still parked behind the old trailer from the Dominguez Circus. But there is a sign glued to the car's rear window: *For Sale. Inquire in the trailer.* Willy Bost knocks on the door as if he were a potential buyer. The little girl opens the door immediately. In her white overalls and blue cap, she looks like a young sailor about to cast off. If he wants to test drive the Chevrolet, he can go for a drive along the lane. She has the keys. He pretends to be interested and goes for a drive.

The little girl is waiting for him impatiently in front of the trailer. When he tells her that he cannot buy the Chevrolet because of a serious problem with the steering, she seems completely dumbfounded. Her grandfather had left for the other side of the ocean, leaving her nothing but the Chevrolet. He did not want to take her along as he had promised, on the pretext that the place he was going is not a place for her. What will she do if she can't sell the Chevrolet because of a serious problem with the steering? She doesn't want to end up at the motel like all the other girls from the Dominguez Circus. There is no question of Willy Bost getting sentimental over the fate of the little girl. He thinks that she is telling him a story, so she won't have to talk about anything else. She does not look like the type to end up at a motel. He asks her about Drove Wrangler. She knows nothing about him, only that he's one of her grandfather's customers. There is no point in insisting. She won't say anything more.

He stops back by the Grand Garage, where Gina Koll is waiting for him, freshly perfumed and made up. Her day is over and she invites him to her place for a drink. She talks energetically. She has a new boss. Drove Wrangler has left San Rosa after selling the Grand Garage to Gobbs.

Willy Bost says nothing. He thinks to himself that Drove Wrangler was careful to put things in order before he left. He also thinks that Gina Koll is surely not just a cashier as she wants him to believe. She lives behind Santa Cruce Church, in a duplex with a view of the towers. The apartment is almost empty, as if she had just moved in, or out. She squeezes up against him. She is more and more provocative. He has only one desire, to take her like he took her in the cabin on the *Moby Dick*. He moans even louder inside her. It is so intense that he can't leave without starting over again, until he can't anymore. Gina Koll is one of those women he can't resist because they predict his desires and fulfill them without holding back. But when he leaves her, he has learned nothing. What she knows she won't tell. Now that he has had all he desired of her, to the point of feeling an emptiness worse than any nausea, he is determined never to see her again.

Commander Roney Burke has spent the day resting and planning his revenge. Willy Bost tells him about his visit to the trailer from the Dominguez Circus. He also tells him that the Grand Garage has been sold to Gobbs. But he says nothing of his adventure with Gina Koll, which took place while he was on duty. Back in the Gold House, after taking off his jacket, he notices that he has lost his notebook. Did he really lose it, or did Gina Koll steal it without his noticing? Now she knows everything he has written in his notebook, and so will whoever it is she is working for. Like an innocent child, he has fallen into her trap.

§19

Mattie is lying next to Nina and Nino. The burial is to take place at eleven o'clock at Santa Cruce. There are flowers everywhere in the ring and the tent is illuminated. All the performers are there, silent and sad. They know they will have no place in Gobbs's plans for the Fuch Circus. Cassy Mac Key is kneeling next to Mattie. She is weeping. And yet she is not a part of the circus, and she never really knew Mattie. She has always tried to be stronger than her pain. And now her pain is pouring out. Cassy remembers Mattie diving into the sea and bringing her back a shell shaped like a conch. She told her it would bring her good luck. They had never spoken of the past, as if it did not exist. But the past came back to kill Mattie. Cassy stops weeping. In memory of Mattie and their meeting at Angel Cove, she swears to do everything in her power never again to be the victim of the past and never again to be the victim of her enemies.

When she approaches Nina and Nino to kiss them for the last time, Lizzie Malik thinks she is hallucinating. How could it be that Livio is back? Even though he has changed, she recognizes him right away. They stay for a long time without speaking, kneeling next to Nino and Nina. Then Livio stands up, and he asks Lizzie to come with him.

He wants to talk to her, even if it is difficult. He tells her everything he told Willy Bost. Lizzie is overwhelmed. The worst thing for her is that Dora Atter used Goppy, the meekest and gentlest one in the circus. She would like to strangle Dora Atter with her own hands for having forced Goppy to cut her rope. What torture his life must have been! She is not angry at Goppy, even if he destroyed her dream of becoming a great acrobat. Of all of them, he is the greatest victim, because he had to live in pain and remorse, with no hope of salvation. Lizzie looks at Livio. She finds it so incredible that he has come back! She no longer feels anything of the great love she once had for him. How everything has changed! She is no longer even angry at the performers of the Fuch Circus for not having supported her after her accident. The only thing that matters to her is taking vengeance on Dora Atter. But how is she to file a complaint against her, when Dora Atter is protected by the law in the person of President Patter? Lizzie in turn tells Livio about her life since the accident. She tells him of her plan to join Father Anders to save the city center. Taking a stand will be a way for her to fight Dora Atter, who destroyed her career.

Suddenly there are flames leaping up toward the heavens. It is the pissotière of the Fuch Circus, which is on fire. In the pissotière, in the middle of the flames, Goppy is swinging at the end of a rope. No one can approach him. The flames make an impassible barrier. When the firemen arrive, Goppy is dead, burned in the pissotière where he hanged himself, and which burned so fast that there now remains nothing more than ashes.

At Santa Cruce, at eleven o'clock, all the performers from the Fuch Circus are sitting side by side in the front rows, petrified by what they have just seen. Lizzie Malik is sitting between Livio and Cassy Mac Key. The three coffins are covered with flowers. The church is full, as it is every time Father Anders gives a sermon. In one corner of the church sits Dora Atter, hidden behind Cidie. The last heir to the Fuch Circus could not avoid coming to the funeral. Father Anders pays a final homage to Nino and Nina, whose act brought laughter and wonder to the people of San Rosa. He also pays homage to Mattie, who made such beautiful costumes, without which the Fuch Circus would never have been what it was. When he has finished his eulogies, his voice changes, and he cries, "Shame be upon the Fuch Circus for having allowed the pissotière to exist in its shadows, like gangrene ready to rot it and kill it!" Father Anders praises the courage of the one who paid for them all by setting fire to it and hanging himself, in expiation for all his sins. He who faced such a death is blessed of God. Hope resides within him and all must honor his memory. "Glory be upon he who dared hang himself after having set fire to the pissotière at the Fuch Circus!" Such is the final sentence of Father Anders's sermon. He staggers as he comes down from the pulpit. He seems to be in the grip of a terrible hallucination, he seems about to die of some fatal blow. Cassy Mac Key trembles after hearing him speak. Father Anders's sermon gives her the strength she needs to do what she has promised. As for Lizzie, she is more determined than ever. To her, taking vengeance on Dora Atter means fighting alongside Father Anders, against all those who have brought gangrene to San Rosa.

Only the performers of the Fuch Circus accompany the coffins to the cemetery. Mattie is buried next to Nino and Nina. The cemetery faces the bay, in the middle of the flowers, just down from the Holy Savior Rest Home. Lizzie Malik and Livio are silent. Lizzie has taken Livio's arm to tell him that she wants to forget the past and that she is happy he has come back to San Rosa.

§20

Dora Atter is in a meeting when Cassy Mac Key asks to see her about signing her contract. Cassy decides to go and wait in her dressing room until Cidie comes for her. A surprise is awaiting her, a wonderful bouquet of roses. There is a card pinned to the bouquet. It is not from Willy Bost, as she had immediately hoped, but from Stive Lenz, whom she met last Sunday atop the volcano. Cassy inhales the scent of the roses. She is suddenly afraid of singing in front of Stive Lenz. He seems so sure of himself and so at ease with everything. What will he think of her songs, in which she speaks of all her pain? But she must be stronger than her fear. Her songs are the weapon she made for herself, all alone, so that she would no longer be afraid.

Dora Atter is finally ready to see her. Cidie shows her into the large office. Cassy Mac Key must speak, since Dora Atter remains silent. She speaks in a tremulous voice which grows surer little by little, pretending that nothing had happened on that first day except for their first meeting. She asks for a three-month contract, with an advance of 50,000 francs. She does not ask for more than three months because she wants to write new songs, which she will not sing at the Babylon. Dora Atter has taken off her dark glasses. Her eyes do not look ill at all. She finds Cassy Mac Key's offer reasonable and has no desire to discuss it. She speaks distantly, with an indifferent air. What happened the first time is not about to happen again, because she no longer thinks about such things. Everything that reminds her of President Hardley must be banished from her memory. From now on her partner is President Patter, who has just officially announced his candidacy for the position of governor, with the support of the Fuller Bank. How could Cassy Mac Key have believed that Dora Atter liked her songs? She thinks that Dora Atter's paralysis is an act, like Cidie's muteness, meant to deceive visitors.

After having been applauded as she is every night, Cassy Mac Key sings her new song, which she has just written in memory of Mattie. When she is finished, the crowd leaves without applauding. They are willing to be moved, but they don't want to hear about what they don't want to know. At the very back of the room, someone shouts bravo. It is Stive Lenz. He takes Cassy Mac Key to dinner at the Bay Blue. He tells her about his film on San Rosa, which he has begun to shoot. His film will include Cassy Mac Key at the Babylon. He is as talkative about his film as about the volcano. He will show San Rosa as it has never before been seen. There will be no professional actors and no script in his film. The actors will be the people of San Rosa and the story will be their stories. But because of the way the film is shot and edited, no one will recognize them. He does not tell Cassy Mac Key about the films he has already made. She thinks that he doesn't talk about them because he wants to forget them. He talks about Tony Landry as if his film were to be a challenge and a revenge. They end the evening walking along the beach. Now Stive Lenz is quiet. He seems very far away all of a sudden.

Back in the Gold House, Cassy Mac Key cannot get to sleep. She can't resist a sudden desire to join Willy Bost in his room. The door is not locked. When she comes in, Willy Bost is already in bed. He does not seem surprised to see her. It is as if he were waiting for her. She undresses without a word. She is trembling, she is so afraid. But afraid of what? When Willy Bost takes her, throwing himself upon her like a madman, it is as if she were losing consciousness. She doesn't even hear his cry, which wakes up Lizzie Malik. The next morning, when she wakes up in her room, she tries to remember what happened during the night with Willy Bost. Because of the marks on her body, she is sure she wasn't dreaming.

§21

Commander Roney Burke has recovered. Now he knows that his time is limited and that he must no longer waste it. He begins his day by putting out to sea on the *Mangor*. He goes as far as the old lighthouse by the reefs. The lighthouse has deteriorated since it was closed down, and sea birds build their nests in it. With his binoculars, the commander surveys the entire bay. The *Salve Regina* is sailing toward Santa Flor. Suddenly a motorboat speeds toward it and stops alongside. The crew of the *Salve Regina* load crates onto the motorboat, which quickly disappears in the direction of Santa Flor, while the *Salve Regina* sets off toward San Rosa. The coast guard is nowhere to be seen. They have orders not to intervene and to stay out of the way when necessary.

Commander Roney Burke wonders why he wants to go on, instead of enjoying the sea aboard the *Mangor*. He could resign. He would go far from San Rosa. He would finally abandon himself to the great pleasure he feels on the sea, far away, farther and farther away from land. He could take on passengers to earn his living and to give him some company. He lies down on the bridge, his eyes closed, to feel himself rocking with the *Mangor*. He thinks of Mattie again, her passion for the depths of the sea. He likes to feel the sea beneath him as he lies on the bridge, but feels no need to come into contact with it. His passion for Rosa Dore seems far away now. Why didn't he simply love her instead of feeling this devouring passion for her? He could have taken her with him out to sea. He would have lain down with her on the bridge, and loved her above the sea and below the sky. If she broke up with him, it must be because he was unable to meet her needs. He is still overwhelmed by Mattie's death, as if she had left him a message as she died. It is a message of love. On the way back to San Rosa, he understands that his passion prevented him from loving, and that passion is love's greatest enemy.

Dany Sapin greets Commander Roney Burke like a friend whose visit he has been awaiting a long time. The *Gazette* is going through a great turning point in its history. Until now, it has been in the service of GobbsBank and the Fuller Bank, which financed it equally. And now, suddenly, Dany Sapin has had a revelation: he must break with GobbsBank and the Fuller Bank and align himself with Father Anders. Standing side by side with Father Anders, Dany Sapin wants to become the figurehead of the opposition, using the *Gazette* to attack the evil that has infected San Rosa.

He hopes to use Father Anders and then eliminate him. He has suddenly developed a personal ambition and wants to have a destiny. In order to make Commander Roney Burke his ally, he warmly invites him to write an article for the *Gazette* on his investigation of the assassination of President Hardley, which all San Rosa has been following.

Commander Roney Burke feels nothing but disdain for Dany Sapin. But he cannot refuse this unhoped-for opportunity to make his voice heard. He will write about what he saw out at sea. But he will not write about his hypotheses on the assassination of President Hardley, because they are only unsubstantiated logical deductions. He does not want the force of logic to replace the truth of facts. Back aboard his boat, he opens the chest in his cabin and takes out his father's revolver, which he has never yet used. It was with this revolver that his father killed himself during the war so he would not be arrested and tortured. Along with the binoculars, the revolver is all he has left of his father.

The commander goes directly to the shooting range. He hits the last target without difficulty, the one that he had missed before, to his great shame. But now that President Patter has also hit the last target, he will have to put one up even farther away, which he will be the only one to hit. Only then will he become the best shot in San Rosa again. He misses the new target. But he will hit it soon if he practices every day. He is sure of that.

On the way to his office, he sees Father Anders's new posters up on walls all over San Rosa. The posters call for a Great Uprising against the orgies of the Babylon and the *Moby Dick*. In very large letters, they say: *Shame be upon those who allow San Rosa to become the city of Shame.* The commander has never been to church in his life. He is proud to be a freethinker. He wonders what could have happened in San Rosa that the head of the opposition, the only one to dare confront the situation and offer solutions, should be this vengeful fanatic with a murky past. There is no question of his supporting Father Anders's candidacy, which he feels to be dangerous. The only thing he will do is to take advantage of Dany Sapin's offer by writing everything he has to say in the *Gazette*. Locked in his office, he writes as he has never written before, in a constant stream, without taking his eyes off the paper. For the first time, he is writing an article, and he will sign it with his own name. He has finally become Commander Roney Burke.

After taking his article to the *Gazette*, the commander stops by the Eden Palace. He cannot go on any longer without seeing Rosa Dore. She is putting up a poster in the lobby. The poster says that she is offering the Eden Palace for sale. She seems happy to see him, as if she had forgotten their breakup. Gobbs has suddenly given up on coproducing Tony Landry's blockbuster. And Tony Landry has suddenly and without explanation broken his contract with Rosa Dore. She did not escape the fate of all those who are romantically linked to Gobbs. He pretended to believe in her film, letting her dream so that he could then break her dream. Rumor has it that Dora Atter immediately became Tony Landry's coproducer. Rosa Dore is putting the Eden Palace up for sale because the Fuller Bank refuses to extend credit to her and to pay her debts from now on. The commander tells her everything that has happened since they broke up. He also tells her about the article that he has just written for the *Gazette*. They go for a walk on the beach. For the first time, the commander brings her aboard the *Mangor*, and shows her his cabin. He has never been so moved. He wants to take her in his arms, but he doesn't dare. He will do it next Sunday, when he takes her out to sea. Then he will love her as he was never able to love her, as if it were the first time.

§22

The electoral campaign has officially begun. Willy Bost went looking for Gina Koll, hoping in vain to get his notebook back. But she has disappeared from the Grand Garage and her duplex is for rent. On the walls of San Rosa there are posters announcing Gobbs's first rally, tonight at eight o'clock, under the tent of the Fuch Circus. President Patter's is planned for ten o'clock at the Babylon. And at midnight, from the top of the highest tower of Santa Cruce, Father Anders will deliver his first campaign address. On the way to join the commander, Willy Bost has never felt so ashamed. He was trapped by Gina Koll like a rank amateur, all because he was unable to resist her advances. And yet he had sworn to himself that he would never again have relations! Last night he fell for it again, this time with Cassy Mac Key! It will never happen again, no, it will never happen again! Starting tonight, he will lock his bedroom door. How humiliating to have to admit his failing to Commander Roney Burke! The commander does not reproach him. He is pleased to see his deputy's pride finally crushed.

The commander and his deputy go to Gobbs's rally. Under the tent, a little behind the podium, sits Gina Koll, un-recognizable in a very severe black suit and tortoiseshell glasses. So she is Gobbs's minion! The rally begins not with a speech but with a video of Goppy, filmed before his death. By stealing Willy Bost's notebook, Gina Koll allowed Gobbs to make use of Goppy. Sobbing, Goppy explains how Dora Atter gave him the order to cut Lizzie Malik's rope. For Lizzie, who is somewhere in the crowd, this is a great moment, when the truth about her accident is finally made public. Gobbs's speech, which follows the film, is full of indignation and anger. How can we trust someone who represents justice in San Rosa but aligns himself with a criminal madwoman? It is no secret that President Patter's candidacy is supported by the Fuller Bank, of which Dora Atter has just been named presi-dent, succeeding President Hardley. Then Gobbs attacks his second adversary. His revelations are very damaging. Father Anders, under the name of Brother John, was the youngest chaplain of the Santa Flor Camp. How, Gobbs cries, could one who hid such an ignominious past be the savior of San Rosa? There is a deathly silence. Commander Roney Burke thinks of his first article, which he was so proud of. And it will appear in Dany Sapin's *Gazette*, which treats this former chaplain of Santa Flor Camp as a hero! His article is tainted.

Next Willy Bost and the commander go to the Babylon, for the second rally of the evening. Like the first, this one does not begin with a speech. The room grows dark and there appear on the screen images filmed aboard the *Moby Dick*. Tony Landry had hidden his cameras there and filmed what no one was ever meant to see. What the images show is enough to destroy Gobbs. He will never become governor of San Rosa now. When the lights come back on, it is not President Patter, still in the shadows, who speaks, but Dora Atter. She denounces Gobbs for pushing Goppy to suicide by forcing him to make this ignoble and false accusation. Then, her voice trembling with emotion, she talks about her accident, which has made her an invalid for life. She has in her possession a letter from Drove Wrangler addressed to President Patter. Before he disappeared forever, ravaged by remorse, Drove Wrangler wanted to denounce himself and to denounce the one who made him a criminal. Gobbs had come to see him one day to ask him to tamper with Dora Atter's car. He wanted her dead so he could buy the Babylon. And it was Gobbs again who asked him to kill President Hardley. Very pale, President Patter succeeds Dora Atter on the podium. He solemnly swears that justice will be done. He will devote his life to giving back to San Rosa the prosperity and happiness that it has so tragically lost.

For the people of San Rosa, overwhelmed by what they have just seen and heard, it is as if the earth were opening up before them. They do not want to believe what Gobbs has revealed to them about Father Anders. They are all waiting for his reply. They are gathered around Santa Cruce waiting for midnight. Only the top of the highest tower, where Father Anders is to appear, is lit. When he appears, everyone is counting on him. He is silent for a long moment. Then he addresses God in a fearsome voice and asks him to destroy San Rosa. Without another word, he throws himself into the void. The Palace Police, hidden in the surrounding streets, emerge and disperse the crowd. To Stive Lenz, who has been filming all of this first night of the campaign, it is a historic evening.

Willy Bost and Commander Roney Burke take a long walk through the deserted streets of San Rosa. What hope is left? The only way out for Gobbs is to flee. President Patter has emerged victorious from this first night of the campaign, since he is the only candidate. Now it is up to him to show that he and he alone will be the true savior of San Rosa. There is a fax waiting for Commander Roney Burke and his deputy. Those in High Places wish to congratulate them on their investigation. The entire police force is searching for Drove Wrangler, President Hardley's assassin, and his arrest is imminent. The investigation is over. The commander informs his deputy of his decision to resign.

Willy Bost has nothing left to wait for. He takes the typewriter from the office and goes back to the Gold House. He writes for the rest of the night. By stealing his notebook, Gina Koll has forced him to write the book that he never wanted to write, for fear that it would take him where he never wanted to go, the Santa Flor Camp where his parents had disappeared forever. He has lived in fear of never coming back from such a trip, like his grandfather who hanged himself one night in the bathroom of the rest home after having finally told him his story. Cassy Mac Key hears him typing all night long. Since the other night, she has been haunted by Willy Bost and can no longer sleep.

Commander Roney Burke goes back to the office alone to consult the archives. He spends the rest of the night rereading his predecessor's files and taking notes so as not to forget anything. Now he understands what he had not understood. Before leaving aboard the *Mangor*, he will write down what his predecessor discovered about the Fuch Circus and the Palace, their secret contacts with the Santa Flor Camp during the war. And he will also write down what he discovered during his investigation of President Hardley. He will not sign his book with his own name, but with his father's nom de guerre, which no one remembers. Commander Roney Burke does not want his predecessor to have died for nothing, and he wants to save the memory of his father, the unknown hero of a terrible time. After having taken all the notes he will need, he has only to leave his office forever and to lock himself in the cabin of the *Mangor*, until he has finished writing his book. Only then will he finally dare ask Rosa Dore to leave with him and start over.

When Willy Bost boards the *Mangor* the next day to talk to the commander about the book he has just begun, the commander is dead, shot through the heart. His father's revolver is lying next to him. There is nothing to explain this act, no letter, no paper, nothing. Willy Bost is sure it was not suicide. But all the evidence says otherwise, so that the truth will never come out. He goes to the office to see if Commander Roney Burke might have left a clue that would help him understand. He finds that the archives have been rifled. The files of Commander Roney Burke's predecessor have disappeared. Willy Bost will never know what the commander learned from them. He goes back to the Gold House and sits down again at his typewriter.

§23

Lizzie Malik is greatly shocked by Father Anders's death and by everything that was revealed about him that night. What troubles her most is that she had let herself be so completely fooled by his sermons, to the point of wanting to support his candidacy, without even trying to find out who he was. How can she fight to save the city center now, and with whose help? It also came as a great shock to her that Goppy, just before hanging himself in the burning pissotière, had revealed to all who Dora Atter was. Lizzie is probably the only one who understands that he did not give in to Gobbs's threats. How could Gobbs's threats hurt him when he had already decided to kill himself after Nino and Nina died? If he gave in to Gobbs, it was to free himself of his torment by accusing Dora Atter, who had ruined his life and destroyed Lizzie Malik's career. But despite the public accusation against Dora Atter, she continues to reign over the Babylon, as if Goppy's confession had gone completely unnoticed. Lizzie sees no more hope for San Rosa.

The death of Father Anders is a terrible shock to all the inhabitants of the city center as well. They no longer believe that anything will ever change for the better. They see only the worst before them. What else is there to do now other than to join President Patter's party? The *Moby Dick* has disappeared from the bay. Now Dora Atter's *Salve Regina* reigns alone, next to the Babylon. The hope that the inhabitants of the city center had felt when they saw the new *Gazette* as their defender is crushed. They are all cursing their gullibility. They believed in Father Anders's words without trying to find out anything about him, as if his words were the word of God. And they believed in Dany Sapin even though they knew who he was. Dany Sapin disappeared from San Rosa after that first night of the campaign. The offices of the *Gazette* are closed for good. A new daily newspaper, the *Battle*, financed by the Fuller Bank, has replaced it. Its director is a young attorney, a close ally of President Patter. Every day, the *Battle* defends the program of the future governor of San Rosa. Lizzie Malik's only comfort is the Gold House. Willy Bost spends almost all his time in his room. Lizzie likes to hear the sound of his typewriter resounding through her house. Willy Bost has been severely affected by the death of Commander Roney Burke. After everything that has happened in San Rosa, the death of Commander Roney Burke has already been forgotten. It was declared a suicide. The office has become nothing more than an answering service. Willy Bost drops by every day to write down the messages, which he then passes on to the Secret Service of the Palace. He has not resigned, because he cannot live without his deputy's salary. He has thrown away much of what he had written. What does he know of the Santa Flor Camp? No trace remains of it. His parents died there like so many others, leaving nothing behind them. He has gone to the site of the old camp several times. Seeing the golfers come and go in the middle of the green lawn, how can one imagine that it was once a death camp? All his grandfather told him about his parents was that they lived only for the circus, where they were acrobats, and that one day they left for the Santa Flor Camp, never to return. He did not even tell him the name of the circus, or where it was located. There were so many back then, and now they have disappeared. How to find it? No matter how much Willy Bost sifts through his memories, he can remember nothing of his parents. He sees only one image, just one, a couple of acrobats taking their bows in the brightly lit ring, and himself, next to his grandfather, shouting bravo. What makes his book so difficult to write is that it is a book of memories written in the absence of memories. He invents his memories as he writes. But the more he writes, the more he discovers that he knows nothing of San Rosa. Each time he throws away what he has written, he doubts that he can go on. But he starts again. He sees no other meaning he might give to his life than to bear witness to what no one wants to know.

Cassy Mac Key continues to sing at the Babylon every night. Is it because she hears Willy Bost's typewriter all day that she has started to write new songs? The new songs are about San Rosa. She takes long walks in the city center. She looks and listens. That is what inspires her songs. She no longer wants to make people cry. She wants to sing songs of anger. She does not know where her anger will lead her. She only needs to express it for the sake of those who will come hear her sing after she leaves the Babylon. She is counting the days until the end of her contract.

Stive Lenz is waiting for President Patter to be elected governor before he finishes his film. That will be on Midsummer Day, and there will be a great celebration in honor of the victory of President Patter. The night Stive Lenz filmed Cassy Mac Key singing at the Babylon was not a night like any other. He took her to dinner at the Bay Blue, like the first time. Then he took her to the top of the volcano on his motorcycle. The moon lights up the bottom of the crater like a spotlight. At the very bottom, the crater is glowing red. As Stive Lenz had predicted, the volcano is slowly awakening. Stive Lenz films the bottom of the crater glowing under the moon, and Cassy Mac Key sitting just at the edge in the dark. Then he puts away his camera and comes and sits down next to her. They could love each other there at the edge of the volcano, but something keeps them from it. They stayed for a long time pressed up against each other looking at the crater, thinking of nothing.

Stive Lenz comes more and more often to spend his evenings at the Gold House, and Rosa Dore as well. Lizzie is happy to have guests in addition to her lodgers. Rosa Dore had hired her at the Eden Palace so that she could restore the Gold House. Now that the Eden Palace is for sale, it is Lizzie's turn to welcome Rosa Dore. She can receive her without shame. She was once the acrobat of the Fuch Circus and her house is the loveliest of the city center. Rosa Dore has not given up on the movies. She is writing a script which will tell the story of her experiences with Commander Roney Burke. Stive Lenz gives her suggestions. He will shoot the film, and she will be the star, as soon as he has finished his film on San Rosa. Her meeting with Stive Lenz is Rosa Dore's second chance at life.

Livio is looking for a space in which to perform as an acrobat. All the performers of the Fuch Circus who want to join him will be welcome. He finally decided on the old train station. It is a train station with sinister memories, through which the trains going to Santa Flor used to pass. Many stopped there, but no one in San Rosa asked any questions about them. The abandoned station is almost in ruins, in the bleakest part of the city center. When Livio asked to buy it, they sold it to him without hesitating. He bought it with the money that Nino and Nina left him as an inheritance. It is also with that money that he hopes to have it restored, to save the memory of the Fuch Circus and of all those anonymous people who passed through the station without knowing where they were going. Cassy Mac Key wants to join with Livio in the development of the space, so that she can sing her new songs there. That is why she has put her coupe up for sale. The money from the sale will be her contribution. But none of the performers from the circus want to join Livio. For them, the story of the Fuch Circus is over. Lizzie wonders if she should try to become an acrobat again. She has had no lasting effects from her accident. Only fear prevents her from starting over. The space will open the night of Midsummer Day celebrations, which will also be the day of the victory of President Patter.

§24

Election day is approaching but there is no excitement, since everyone knows that President Patter will be elected governor. Throughout San Rosa, posters announce the Midsummer Day festivities. The Babylon will offer free admission. Tony Landry's movies will be shown nonstop. Dora Atter will be queen of the festival. She will finally have what she has always wanted, to become the wife of the governor of San Rosa. President Patter will offer what President Hardley never granted her. Such is the contract she signed with him. To celebrate Midsummer Day, there will be bonfires along the bay, and there will be fireworks shot off from the lighthouse. The people of San Rosa are preparing for the festival without giving a thought to the elections.

That evening, Cassy Mac Key will finally have finished at the Babylon. For the first time, she will sing her new songs in Livio's space, which will become her own. Now it has a name, the Nevermore. It was Willy Bost who came up with the idea, from the title he wants to give his book, if he ever manages to write it: *Nevermore*. Work has begun on the Nevermore. For Midsummer Day, they will have to put up a ring, a stage, and seats in the middle of the worksite. Lizzie Malik has begun to train herself as an acrobat again, in secret. She has lost the grace she once had. But she is gaining confidence little by little as she remembers her old routines. When Livio surprised her as she was practicing, he was amazed. He immediately suggested that she work with him. Their first act will be ready for Midsummer Day. Rehearsing is their only concern. Lizzie has rediscovered the joy of being an acrobat, without trying to outdo herself as she used to. What matters is the act that Livio and she are inventing together. Livio is no longer the man she was madly in love with in the days of the Fuch Circus. Now he is her partner at the Nevermore, with whom she will become an acrobat again, after having thought that it was over forever.

As expected, President Patter is elected governor of San Rosa, with an absolute majority. For the opening of the Nevermore, Lizzie Malik invites her grandmother and Sister Cize. It would not be a real festival for her if her grandmother were not there. Her grandmother is returning to the Gold House for the first time since she left it to go and live in the rest home. Seeing it so carefully restored, she thinks she is in a fairy tale. Now she wants to sing all her repertoire from the old days. That is how Lizzie learns that her grandmother was a singer in a music hall in San Rosa, since disappeared, called the Gold House. Helped by Sister Cize, her grandmother remembers all her songs and is finding her voice again, even if it is a little shaky. She voted for President Patter because everyone likes him at the Holy Savior Rest Home, since he pledged to look after the home personally. He went to visit every lodger and promised to carry out their wishes. But for Midsummer Day, she wants to be at the Nevermore, not at the Babylon. After seeing Livio and Lizzie's last rehearsal, Sister Cize thanks God for having performed such a miracle. To bring luck to Cassy Mac Key, Lizzie gives her Nina's notebook full of songs. Cassy is learning to sing them. She will sing them along with her new songs, in memory of Nina.

When the doors of the Nevermore open for the first time, Livio and Lizzie are at the entry to greet their guests for the night. There are very old people, who have come to see her grandmother, and there are also former spectators from the Fuch Circus who admired Lizzie and Livio back when the Fuch Circus was still the Fuch Circus. The regulars at Gobbs's Amusement Park have all gone to the big party at the Babylon. Willy Bost is sitting alone, in the last row. Everything seems unreal to him, even the Nevermore. As if he were deaf, he can't listen to Cassy Mac Key's new songs, and he has a dark veil over his eyes when Lizzie Malik does her act with Livio. He is thinking about his book, which he no longer believes in. The truth about San Rosa, like the truth about Santa Flor, escapes him. He has the impression that his words lead to nothing but a black hole in which he is lost. How could he have hoped he would succeed, when he has never been able to finish what he began? Now he knows that it is not only the fault of those in High Places. It is the fault of his central collapse, into which he sinks every time. The grandmother has just finished taking her bows when a violent explosion resounds through the building. The lights suddenly go out. Willy Bost takes advantage of the dark to leave unnoticed. Bewildered, he walks toward the ocean.

It is as if the end of the world had come. A bomb has just exploded at the Babylon, in the room where Tony Landry's movies were being shown. At the same moment, the bay is illuminated by all the Midsummer Day bonfires, while in the middle of the ocean, set off from the lighthouse, the fireworks have begun. In the middle of the bay the fishing boats from Gobbs's fleet are grouped in a circle around the *Moby Dick*, which has mysteriously reappeared. At the same moment, the volcano finally reawakens and launches its own fireworks toward the heavens, while lava flows down the slopes of the volcano, burning everything in its path. From the *Moby Dick*, Gobbs can watch the destruction of the Babylon and of his Amusement Park

at the same time. The tent of the Fuch Circus is in
flames. Stive Lenz is running from place to place filming
everything he sees, as if this were one of Tony Landry's
blockbusters. Sirens from fire trucks and special service
cars are blaring everywhere.

President Patter calls together his council for an emergency
meeting. Afterward, he gives a long speech, broadcast
simultaneously on the channels of San Rosa and Santa
Flor. It was not a bomb at the Babylon, but an accidental
explosion caused by a general short circuit. The story of
the short circuit excuses him from having to look for
a culprit. Dora Atter has died in the explosion, along
with Cidie. President Patter says nothing more about
Dora Atter. Everyone understands that she will never be
mentioned again in San Rosa. Lizzie Malik will be able to
live in peace. The one who wanted to kill her is dead and
nothing will survive her. President Patter urges everyone
to remain calm and to be brave. The Volcano area, the
only part of town to have been destroyed by the eruption,
will be rebuilt. His thoughts are with the victims and the
victims' families. They will all receive a settlement. Now
it is necessary to prepare for the future of San Rosa and
to forget this incident. The president praises the rescue
teams who, at the risk of their own lives, helped to avoid
a catastrophe. The volcano has already gone quiet. The
volcanologists are all in agreement that this is the last
eruption of the volcano of San Rosa and that it will now

take its place in the chain of extinct volcanoes. The reign of President Patter has just begun. His address to San Rosa is considered worthy and courageous. He is a man who knows how to face difficult events and to find the right words. San Rosa is proud to have him as its governor. The destruction of the Babylon and the Amusement Park is necessary if San Rosa is to be reconstructed on a different foundation.

The grandmother listened to President Patter's long speech without understanding it. The only thing she grasped was that the Holy Savior Rest Home had been completely destroyed by the lava flow and that the president mourns the dead as if they were his own family. Sister Cize and the grandmother are the only survivors. The grandmother will spend her last days at the Gold House. She thanks God for having brought her back to her house and her songs, at the very moment that Lizzie became an acrobat again and found Livio again. As for Sister Cize, she wants to sign on with the Nevermore and donate whatever services she can. She is overwhelmed by everything that has just happened. She has lost her faith in God. If God existed, He would never have let the volcano destroy the Holy Savior Rest Home, where all the lodgers were burned to death in their beds.

Willy Bost has left the Gold House to live on the *Mangor*. Every day, he puts out to sea. He has given up on finishing his book and wants to forget everything. The commander gave him the most precious gift possible by leaving him his boat. The Pontiac is parked on the dock. Willy Bost never uses it anymore. Cassy Mac Key did not stay long at the Gold House after Willy Bost's departure. She rented a studio near the Nevermore. She likes the abandoned neighborhood and is not afraid to live there. The inhabitants come and listen to her sing. Her songs tell them about themselves, but they don't know it. She is proud to sing at the Nevermore every night. Even if she sings to a very small crowd, it is a real crowd. The inhabitants of the city center are coming to the Nevermore in increasing numbers, drawn there by word of mouth. For the first time since she was released from prison, she is not ashamed, and she feels freed from the past. She is keeping the promise she made the day Mattie was buried. The hardest thing for her is not to think about Willy Bost, from whom she has heard nothing. His absence possesses her despite herself, even when she is singing.

§25

The Fuller Bank, which was sent into an upheaval with Dora Atter's death, has just merged with GobbsBank. The Gobbs & Fuller Company now reigns over Santa Flor and San Rosa. Livio lost half the money from his inheritance, which he had invested in shares of the Fuller Bank. To restore the Nevermore, he will have to borrow money at a high interest rate because Gobbs & Fuller has decided to charge different interest rates to different sorts of customers. Rosa Dore has sold the Eden Palace for far less than it was worth. She made hardly enough to pay her debts. The same person bought Rosa Dore's Eden Palace and Cassy Mac Key's coupe, which also went for far less than it was worth. The new owner is Gina Koll, who has reappeared in San Rosa with a fortune she made – no one knows how – on the other side of the border. She is planning to have major work done on the Eden Palace. The time of Gina Koll's Eden Palace is coming.

Gobbs has also reappeared. He sued Dora Atter posthumously for libel, and won. Drove Wrangler's letter accusing him of a double crime was a forgery. Now Gobbs can live in San Rosa with his head held high. The Volcano area is undergoing reconstruction. There is nothing to prevent this because the volcano was officially declared dead by the volcanologists of San Rosa. Gobbs has decided to give up on rebuilding his Amusement Park. The time of the Amusement Park, like the time of the Babylon, is past, along with that of the Fuch Circus. Now Gobbs wants to create a Park of Arts and Letters in San Rosa. President Patter has forgotten what made him oppose Gobbs so violently on that memorable first night of the electoral campaign. Gobbs, whose enterprising spirit and devotion to San Rosa are endlessly praised in the pages of the *Battle*, has been appointed to the Palace Council, in which he holds the position, specially created for him, of Minister of Arts and Letters in charge of Social Affairs. As for Gina Koll, she has just been named director of the San Rosa Cinema Festival. Inaugurating this festival was the idea of the Lossfell Company, and it was immediately approved by the Palace. Tony Landry, currently filming his new blockbuster, will undoubtedly win the Gold Medal.

The *Battle* constantly tells of Gobbs's plans for the Park of Arts and Letters. Special fellowships will be set up for artists who propose new projects. A Residence Hall, built in the middle of the Park, will house the fellows. The *Battle* also tells every day of the great fight that has begun against the poverty and dilapidation of the city center. Shelters are being set up, financed by the families in the Bay area. Mutual aid teams, made up of young people, make house calls to look after the most unfortunate inhabitants. In his Sunday chronicle, the director of the *Battle* speaks of the combat that must be undertaken to reestablish the values of family and faith, the groundwork of a new social justice. Culture, exemplified by Gobbs's new Park, will be a decisive weapon in this combat. Culture must be a duty for each of us and the right of all.

Stive Lenz and Rosa Dore came to the Gold House to say their goodbyes. Stive Lenz is about to start a tour to publicize his film on San Rosa, which has just received a special prize from the Lossfell Company. The last eruption of the volcano, the burning of the Fuch Circus, and the explosion of the Babylon, which appear at the end of the film, are unforgettable images and guarantee its success. Stive Lenz has asked Rosa Dore to accompany him on the tour. A new career is beginning for him. Rosa Dore has never left San Rosa. Thanks to Stive Lenz, she will finally see the world. When they get back, she will appear in Stive Lenz's new film, for which she has just finished the script. It's a new version of *Eden Palace*, which will bring back Commander Roney Burke and President Hardley, under different names. But the Eden Palace as Gina Koll has restored it no longer looks like the Eden Palace. Stive Lenz will have it rebuilt in the studios of the Lossfell Company for the filming.

Cassy Mac Key envies Rosa Dore for having the good luck to be loved by Stive Lenz just as he is beginning a second career, with the support of Lossfell. For her, it is not so easy to begin life anew. To make herself stronger when she feels discouraged, she tries to follow the example of Lizzie Malik. Lizzie lives for the Gold House which she had restored and for the Nevermore where she has become an acrobat again alongside Livio. How could she have been so lucky as to reconstruct her whole life? Cassy Mac Key thinks it is because of the Gold House which her grandmother bought for Lizzie so that she would have an inheritance, and also because of the Fuch Circus, whose memory she and Livio are rescuing. What she herself is lacking is an inheritance and a memory. That was what brought her so close to Willy Bost. He has no inheritance either, and his memory is the lost memory of the Santa Flor Camp. Singing every night at the Nevermore is her only reason to live, and yet it is no longer enough.

Cassy Mac Key has fallen into the habit of going to swim at Angel Cove. Nothing is left of Mattie's buvette. She has lost her fear of never surfacing when she dives underwater. It was by diving all the way to the bottom of the cove that she discovered the grotto Mattie had told her about. At the very end of this very deep grotto, there is an extraordinary sight, the complete skeleton of an enormous whale. The whale must have come there to die, as if that were the cemetery it had chosen. So this was the hidden treasure of Angel Cove, which Mattie so wanted to show her. Cassy stays for hours at the far end of the grotto looking at the skeleton of the whale. Some days when she feels very sad, she tells herself that she could go to sleep there near the whale, and never wake up.

It is on a Sunday when he has landed at Angel Cove that Willy Bost runs into Cassy Mac Key, whom he has not seen since Midsummer Day. She wrote him, but he never answered. They are both very embarrassed by this unexpected meeting. Cassy Mac Key is the first to break the silence. She tells Willy Bost that she has something to show him. They dive together down to the grotto. She leads him to the very end, to the skeleton of the whale.

They stay for a long time, motionless and silent, looking at it.

A few days later, the *Mangor* was discovered drifting in the middle of the reefs. There was no one on board. As for Cassy Mac Key, she has never reappeared at the Nevermore. We will never know what happened between Cassy Mac Key and Willy Bost in the grotto. Ever since Mattie's death, Angel Cove has become a cursed place, which everyone wants to forget, and where no one ever goes.

In the European Women Writers series